Katie O'Brien

POEMS OF THE SEA

POEMS OF THE SEA

With an introduction by
ADAM NICOLSON

Edited by
GABY MORGAN

MACMILLAN COLLECTOR'S LIBRARY

This collection first published 2021 by Macmillan Collector's Library
an imprint of Pan Macmillan
The Smithson, 6 Briset Street, London EC1M 5NR
EU representative: Macmillan Publishers Ireland Limited,
Mallard Lodge, Lansdowne Village, Dublin 4
Associated companies throughout the world
www.panmacmillan.com

ISBN 978-1-5290-4566-6

Introduction copyright © Adam Nicolson 2021
Selection and arrangement copyright © Macmillan Publishers International Limited 2021

The permissions acknowledgements on p. 243
constitute an extension of this copyright page.

1 3 5 7 9 8 6 4 2

A CIP catalogue record for this book is available from the British Library.

Cover and endpaper design: Mel Four, Pan Macmillan Art Department
Typeset in Plantin by Jouve (UK), Milton Keynes
Printed and bound in China by Imago

MIX
Paper from
responsible sources
FSC® C116313
www.fsc.org

Visit **www.panmacmillan.com** to read more
about all our books and to buy them.

For Grant, Jude and Evie

Contents

SONG OF THE BROOK

WILD NIGHTS!

THE LAKE ISLE OF INNISFREE

THE JUMBLIES

Introduction

Adam Nicolson

The poet Alice Oswald has said recently that 'the surface of water is complicated by transparency, and its transparency is complicated by refraction . . . The physics or nature of water is metaphysical, meaning that its surface expresses more than itself.'

That is water's allure: it can always mean more than itself. It is a substance in the world and yet its meaning, or the meanings it can carry, are as elusive as meaning in music. When Schumann was asked what one of his compositions meant, his answer was to play it again. In music, meaning and being are inextricable – it means what it is – and water shares that quality. It is only itself and yet inevitably more than itself. It is the most layered thing in our daily life. If we could see the air, we would think the same of it, but water uniquely in the physical world fuses opaqueness with transparency; we see what it is and have no idea what it is. Is it any surprise that it is the great medium for poetry?

Perhaps there is something else in play. Half of all the water in the world, half of all the rivers, lakes and seas, was made before the world began. For billions of years after the universe jumped into being, shock waves from star formation bound together the hydrogen and oxygen atoms that were adrift between the stars. Most of that water still floats across the universe in giant molecular clouds, not unlike the vast streaming rivers of water that transpire from tropical rain forests and flow above them to fall as life-giving rain beyond their borders. 'The

Orion Nebula in our galaxy creates enough water every day to fill the world's ocean sixty times over,' the polymath Caspar Henderson has written. There are billions of planets largely or wholly covered in water, 'either frozen solid or rolling in global oceans tens or even hundreds of kilometres deep.'

I often wonder if we have some intuition of this; when we stand on a beach or allow ourselves to drift downstream with the current of a river, or feel suddenly alive when casting off from a quay, raising the sails and allowing the boat to move out beyond the headlands, do we then have some recognition that this is the most elemental of experiences, as deep and cosmic an encounter with reality as entering the dark of a rock fissure or a cave, where the ordinariness of life is just as completely suspended?

All the poems in this anthology recognize, on the surface or not, this otherness of water. Or at least its combination of the primordial and the familiar. And of all the poets of water – leave aside for a moment Shakespeare's life-long entrancement with the sea – there is none that touches me more than Tennyson. Water for him is everything: the sea itself, its edges, the crossing of those edges, the rocky shore, the tangled margins of a lake, the dark surface of a pool over which mist rises on cold mornings that feel like the beginning or the end of the world, the uncertain sources of a brook in the 'haunts of coot and hern' – all become for him the most plangent elements of a giant metaphorical landscape in which love, longing, loss, sorrow, beauty, nobility and the desire for the mystic and the strange find their richest poetic home.

'Crossing the Bar' is his final water statement. The ancient poet confronts the prospect of life making its turn out into the ocean, a movement so inevitable and so huge that the tide that will take him away 'seems asleep, / Too full for sound and foam, / When that which drew from out the boundless deep / Turns again home.'

The words are private, almost hesitant, meditative, a man alone on a shore he knows he will never know again, but also sonorous, the voice of a prophet, speaking from personal wisdom in the knowledge that his understanding is for all of us. The lines carry echoes from the *Morte d'Arthur*, written sixty years earlier and among the most beautiful water poems in the language, omitted from this collection only for reasons of length. It is one of Tennyson's many elegies for Arthur Hallam, a man he had loved more than anyone on earth and who had died whilst abroad aged twenty-two. Tennyson transmuted Arthur Hallam into the Dark Age king who in the poem lay dying after the final battle, and who Sir Bedivere, the last of all his knights, took

> to a chapel nigh the field,
> A broken chancel with a broken cross,
> That stood on a dark strait of barren land.
> On one side lay the ocean, and on one
> Lay a great water, and the moon was full.

Everything a water landscape might become is here, a place 'where lay the mighty bones of ancient men, / Old knights, and over them the sea-wind sang / Shrill, chill, with flakes of foam' . . . 'a waste land, where no one comes, / Or hath come, since the making of the world.' And there, on the waters of 'the level lake', under 'the long glories of the winter moon', Tennyson's Arthur is taken by the three strange Queens of death onto the dark barge that

Moved from the brink, like some full-breasted swan
That, fluting a wild carol ere her death,
Ruffles her pure cold plume, and takes the flood
With swarthy webs.

T. S. Eliot called Tennyson 'the saddest of all English poets', and it may be that his natural melancholy found in water the medium that was most responsive to a sense of uncertainty, a floatingness, of the world and our life no more than half-tethered to anything sure. Water may be entrancing for the sense of possibility that waits in every molecule, but it is daunting for the same reason: you cannot know where you are with it, 'as if swaying were its form of stillness', as D. H. Lawrence wrote of seaweed and might just as well have said of water itself.

Without warning, this anxiety can turn on its head. All the jack-tar adventurousness that comes swinging out in the brio and swagger of the sea shanties here, the sheer delight in raising the anchor and easing the sheets, the world inhabited by 'the master, the swabber, the boatswain and I, / The gunner and his mate,' is only the other side of this liquidity of water. The sea-world is a world to be lived in. Everything is possible there. It is the spirit alive in John Masefield's 'wheel's kick and the wind's song and the white sail's shaking' and it is in the great hymn to the voyage made by Columba or Colum Cille, the Dove of the Church, sailing from Ireland to Iona in the seventh or eighth century:

He brings northward to meet the Lord a bright crowd
* of chancels –*
Colum Cille, kirks for hundreds, widespread candle . . .
He crossed the wave-strewn wild region, foam-flecked,
* seal-filled,*
Savage, bounding, seething, white-tipped, pleasing, doleful.

That energy of what Homer called 'the unfenced sea' is the energy of life itself. But it is also its destructiveness. Every part of the sea that gives you life will also give you death. That is the tension at the heart of every sea poem, from the *Odyssey* onwards. And it surges up again and again in Shakespeare. Timon of Athens is a tyrant whose idea of himself is a noble, constant and generous man, 'not of that feather to shake off / My friend when he must need me', but he comes to the end of his life disgusted with the shifting hypocrisies of men. He loathes people and all their works. And so, in the self-dramatizing and self-referential way of the Shakespearean hero, he has his tomb made not in the security of dry land but on the very edge of the tide, 'where the light foam of the sea may beat / [His] gravestone daily'. 'Come not to me again, but say to Athens,' he announces to his followers, that he

> hath made his everlasting mansion
> Upon the beached verge of the salt flood;
> Who once a day with his embossed froth
> The turbulent surge shall cover.

The words mimic the trouble of the place his body will lie: not an everlasting mansion but a tumultuous shore, full of the breaking of the surf, alive with unrest. As Alice Oswald has said, 'the sea in its dark psychosis dreams of your death.'

There are some who have not liked Matthew Arnold's 'Dover Beach' – Robert Frost among them – because it does not approach the world with the gaiety or optimism that they require. But it is one I love, not least for the sea music that runs through it, its fusion of the still water in the Channel lying quiet beneath the moon with the longer and deeper undersong of the surf dragging again and again at the 'naked shingles of the world'. The two are one: the 'turbid ebb and flow' lies within the stillness.

In that way, Arnold's sea speaks in many simultaneous voices. It is a straightforward depiction of the beauty of the Channel at night, but also an elegy for certainty and even happiness. The poet's hopes and expectations for the love between him and his bride seem infinitely fragile when confronted with the faithless future of this sea. The two of them gazing out into the moonlit dark are afloat on what Shakespeare in *The Tempest* calls 'sea-sorrow', the melancholy at the heart of a changing world. Brightness has gone. Now there is only night-wind to accompany their thoughts. All through their anxieties and meditations, the sea continues to break, the surf coming and going like doubt itself, or at least like the dialogue between hope and doubt, giving and taking, surging and withdrawing, to leave the stones of the naked shingle bright and wet in the moonlight.

I don't know a poem in which the physical world is made to appear so sentient, as if the sea and its shore were alive to the troubles of life on its surface. Like the greatest of sea poems, 'Dover Beach' makes present all the transformations possible in the poetry of water, the recognition of life's beauty, always accompanied by the eternal note of sadness as, in the words of T. S. Eliot, we 'wear white flannel trousers, and walk upon the beach,' listening to 'the mermaids singing, each to each.'

SEA FEVER:
THE SEA

Rhyme Scheme: AABB

Ballad

The person wants to go sailing again & feel the wind, & tides & see all the animals, oceans, etc. The ocean is "calling them" to sail again. They want to live on the sea & have a ~~g~~ merry time. They want to relax on the ocean.

Theme: Living Life to the Fullest

"Vagrant gypsy life." (lines 15-16)

This reminds me of a song called, "The Call," which is about God calling us to awaken in the spirit. ~~If God calls us we should follow him~~. If God calls us, we should follow like we have ~~Spi~~ "Holy Spirit fever".

hexameter

longing

lyrical waves

winds & sea

Refrain

Sea Fever

A I must down to the seas again, to the lonely sea and
the sky, *(personification)*

A And all I ask is a tall ship and a star to steer her by; *(helm symbolism)*

B And the wheel's kick and the wind's song and the
white sail's shaking, *(personification)*

B And a grey mist on the sea's face, and a grey dawn
breaking. *(personification)* *(imagery)*

A I must down to the seas again, for the call of the
running tide

A Is a wild call and a clear call that may not be denied; *(personification)*

B And all I ask is a windy day with the white clouds
flying, *(imagery)*

B And the flung spray and the blown spume, and the
sea-gulls crying. *(imagery)* *(foam)*

A I must down to the seas again, to the vagrant gypsy
life, *(wandering)*

A To the gull's way and the whale's way where the
wind's like a whetted knife; *(simile)* *(alliteration)* *(imagery)*

B And all I ask is a merry yarn from a laughing
fellow-rover, *(imagery, personification)*

B And quiet sleep and a sweet dream when the long
trick's over. *(imagery)*

John Masefield (1878–1967)

Ocean is
mesmerizing

Sailors

trick-assigned
schedule

an accompanying
wanderer; fellow
travelling companion

3

Sea Longing

A thousand miles beyond this sun-steeped wall
    Somewhere the waves creep cool along the sand,
    The ebbing tide forsakes the listless land
With the old murmur, long and musical;
The windy waves mount up and curve and fall,
    And round the rocks the foam blows up like snow –
    Tho' I am inland far, I hear and know,
For I was born the sea's eternal thrall.
I would that I were there and over me
    The cold insistence of the tide would roll,
    Quenching this burning thing men call the soul, –
Then with the ebbing I should drift and be
    Less than the smallest shell along the shoal,
Less than the seagulls calling to the sea.

Sara Teasdale (1884–1933)

Exultation is in the Going

Exultation is in the going
Of an inland soul to sea,
Past the houses—past the headlands—
Into deep Eternity—

Bred as we, among the mountains,
Can the sailor understand
The divine intoxication
Of the first league out from land?

Emily Dickinson (1830–1886)

from Romeo and Juliet

(Act 2 Scene 2 lines 133–5)

My bounty is as boundless as the sea,
My love as deep; the more I give to thee,
The more I have: for both are infinite.

William Shakespeare (1564–1616)

It's the Sea I Want

It's the sea I want,
Make no mistake,
Not the resorts
With boardinghouses
Pressed together and shivering,
Praying for sun
And central heating –
It's the sea I want,
The whole boiling,
Destructive, disruptive, sterilising –
I think it's smashing
Undermining
This island,
Unpinning
Gorse and headland,
Arresting, without warrant,
Growth and sunlight.
Landscapes at risk,
Thumped with fists of wind,
Eaten up with a mouthful of mist,
Slump like a Stock Market
Suddenly into the Channel.
Down the long final slide
Go houses full of the dying,
Carefully tended gardens
Into the riot of salt . . .
While
All along
A population of cold

Shelled and speechless creatures
Waits, to inherit
The hot, hideous, restless
Chaos I've helped to make
In sixty industrious years.
Sixy industrious years
And the motorway from the Midlands
Have brought me down at last
To the level of the sea.
I see with the sea's eye.
It bites the cliffs,
Fondles the coats, and swings
Away again, out to sea,
Waving, waving,
Making no promises,
It spits back in our faces
The coins and cans of the beaches.
It's the sea I want,
Belting the land, breaking
All the rules, speaking
Its guttural, thrusting tongue.
It pays no taxes,
Cringes before no conscience
And carries its own prestige
On its naked, shining back.
It's the sea I want,
If it's not too late
To sit, and contemplate
The hard bright barbarous jewels
Of the totally indifferent sea:
Something I never made
And cannot be guilty of.

I have done with the pains of love.
Leave me alone with the sea,
That picks bones clean,
And was, and shall be.

Elma Mitchell (1919–2000)

Mana of the Sea

Do you see the sea, breaking itself to bits against
      the islands
yet remaining unbroken, the level great sea?

Have I caught from it
the tides in my arms
that runs down to the shallows of my wrists,
      and breaks
abroad in my hands, like waves among the rocks
      of substance?

Do the rollers of the sea
roll down my thighs
and over the submerged islets of my knees
with power, sea-power
sea-power
to break against the ground
in the flat, recurrent breakers of my two feet?

And is my body ocean, ocean
whose power runs to the shores along my arms
and breaks in the foamy hands, whose power rolls out
to the white-treading waves of two salt feet?

I am the sea, I am the sea!

D. H. Lawrence (1885–1930)

Song of the Sea

Timeless sea breezes,
sea-wind of the night:
you come for no one;
if someone should wake,
he must be prepared
how to survive you.

Timeless sea breezes,
that for aeons have
blown ancient rocks,
you are purest space
coming from afar . . .

Oh, how a fruit-bearing
fig tree feels your coming
high up in the moonlight.

Rainer Maria Rilke (1875–1926)

Anchored

If thro' the sea of night which
      here surrounds me,
I could swim out beyond the
      farthest star,
Break every barrier of circumstance
      that bounds me,
And greet the Sun of sweeter
      life afar,

Tho' near you there is passion,
      grief, and sorrow,
And out there rest and joy and
      peace and all,
I should renounce that beckoning
      for to-morrow,
I could not choose to go beyond
      your call.

Paul Laurence Dunbar (1872–1906)

from Don Juan

V

The wind swept down the Euxine, and the wave
> Broke foaming o'er the blue Symplegades;
'Tis a grand sight from off the 'Giant's Grave'
> To watch the progress of those rolling seas
Between the Bosphorus, as they lash and lave
> Europe and Asia, you being quite at ease;
There's not a sea the passenger e'er pukes in,
> Turns up more dangerous breakers than the
> Euxine.

George Gordon, Lord Byron (1788–1824)

The Tide Rises, the Tide Falls

The tide rises, the tide falls,
The twilight darkens, the curlew calls;
Along the sea-sands damp and brown
The traveller hastens toward the town,
    And the tide rises, the tide falls.

Darkness settles on roofs and walls,
But the sea, the sea in the darkness calls;
The little waves, with their soft, white hands,
Efface the footprints in the sands,
    And the tide rises, the tide falls.

The morning breaks; the steeds in their stalls
Stamp and neigh, as the hostler calls;
The day returns, but nevermore
Returns the traveller to the shore,
    And the tide rises, the tide falls.

Henry Wadsworth Longfellow (1807–1882)

Strange Sea

Implausible fish bloom in the depths,
mercurial flowers light up the coast:
I know red and yellow, the other colors, –
But the sea, *det granna granna havet*, that's most
    dangerous
to look at.
What name is there for the color that arouses
this thirst, which says,
the saga can happen, even to you –

Edith Södergran (1892–1923) tr. Averill Curdy

Ariel's Song

Full fathom five thy father lies,
    Of his bones are coral made:
Those are pearls that were his eyes,
    Nothing of him that doth fade,
But doth suffer a sea-change
Into something rich, and strange:
Sea-nymphs hourly ring his knell –
    Hark! now I hear them,
        Ding-dong bell.

William Shakespeare (1564–1616)

All Day I Hear the Noise of Waters

All day I hear the noise of waters
    Making moan,
Sad as the sea-bird is, when going
    Forth alone,
He hears the winds cry to the waters'
    Monotone.

The grey winds, the cold winds are blowing
    Where I go.
I hear the noise of many waters
    Far below.
All day, all night, I hear them flowing
    To and fro.

James Joyce (1882–1941)

Break, Break, Break

Break, break, break,
    On thy cold gray stones, O Sea!
And I would that my tongue could utter
    The thoughts that arise in me.

O, well for the fisherman's boy,
    That he shouts with his sister at play!
O, well for the sailor lad,
    That he sings in his boat on the bay!

And the stately ships go on
    To their haven under the hill;
But O for the touch of a vanished hand,
    And the sound of a voice that is still!

Break, break, break,
    At the foot of thy crags, O Sea!
But the tender grace of a day that is dead
    Will never come back to me.

Alfred, Lord Tennyson (1809–1892)

Sea-Change

You are no more, but sunken in a sea
Sheer into dream, ten thousand leagues, you fell;
And now you lie green-golden, while a bell
Swings with the tide, my heart; and all is well
Till I look down, and wavering, the spell –
Your loveliness – returns. There in the sea,
Where you lie amber-pale and coral-cool,
You are most loved, most lost, most beautiful.

Genevieve Taggard (1894–1948)

The World Below the Brine

The world below the brine;
Forests at the bottom of the sea – the branches
    and leaves,
Sea lettuce, vast lichens, strange flowers and seeds –
    the thick tangle, openings, and pink turf,
Different colors, pale gray and green, purple, white
    and gold – the play of light through the water,
Dumb swimmers there among the rocks – coral,
    gluten, grass, rushes, and the aliment of the
    swimmers,
Sluggish existences grazing there suspended,
    or slowly crawling close to the bottom,
The sperm-whale at the surface, blowing air and spray,
    or disporting with his flukes,
The leaden-eyed shark, the walrus, the turtle, the hairy
    sea-leopard, and the sting-ray;
Passions there – wars, pursuits, tribes – sight in those
    ocean-depths, breathing that thick-breathing air,
    as so many do;
The change thence to the sight here, and to the subtle
    air breathed by beings like us who walk
    this sphere,
The change onward from ours to that of beings
    who walk other spheres.

Walt Whitman (1819–1892)

Under the Surface

On the surface, foam and roar,
    Restless heave and passionate dash,
Shingle rattle along the shore,
    Gathering boom and thundering crash.

Under the surface, soft green light,
    A hush of peace and endless calm,
Winds and waves from a choral height,
    Falling sweet as a far-off psalm.

On the surface, swell and swirl,
    Tossing weed and drifting waif,
Broken spars that the mad waves whirl,
    Where wreck-watching rocks they chafe.

Under the surface, loveliest forms.
    Feathery fronds with crimson curl,
Treasures too deep for the raid of storms,
    Delicate coral and hidden pearl.

On the surface, lilies white,
    A painted skiff with a singing crew,
Sky-reflections soft and bright,
    Tremulous crimson, gold and blue.

Under the surface, life in death,
    Slimy tangle and oozy moans,
Creeping things with watery breath,
    Blackening roots and whitening bones.

On the surface, a shining reach,
     A crystal couch for the moonbeams' rest,
Starry ripples along the beach,
     Sunset songs from breezy west.

Under the surface, glooms and fears,
     Treacherous currents swift and strong,
Deafening rush in the drowning ears, –
     Have ye rightly read my song?

Frances Ridley Havergal (1836–1879)

The Ocean

The Ocean has its silent caves,
Deep, quiet, and alone;
Though there be fury on the waves,
Beneath them there is none.

The awful spirits of the deep
Hold their communion there;
And there are those for whom we weep,
The young, the bright, the fair.

Calmly the wearied seamen rest
Beneath their own blue sea.
The ocean solitudes are blest,
For there is purity.

The earth has guilt, the earth has care,
Unquiet are its graves;
But peaceful sleep is ever there,
Beneath the dark blue waves.

Nathaniel Hawthorne (1804–1864)

from Childe Harold's Pilgrimage

And I have loved thee, Ocean! and my joy
Of youthful sports was on the breast to be
Borne, like thy bubbles, onward; from a boy
I wantoned with thy breakers, – they to me
Were a delight; and if the freshening sea
Made them a terror, 't was a pleasing fear;
For I was as it were a child of thee,
And trusted to thy billows far and near,
And laid my land upon thy mane, – as I do here.

George Gordon, Lord Byron (1788–1824)

SHE SELLS SEA SHELLS:
THE SEASHORE

Sea Shell

Sea Shell, Sea Shell,
     Sing me a song, O Please!
A song of ships and pirate men,
     And parrots, and tropical trees.

Of islands lost in the Spanish Main
Which no man may ever find again,
Of fishes and corals under the waves,
And sea-horses stabled in great green caves.

Sea Shell, Sea Shell,
Sing of the things you know so well.

Amy Lowell (1874–1925)

The Shell

1 And then I pressed the shell
2 Close to my ear, *imagery*
3 And listened well.

4 And straightaway, like a bell, *simile*
5 Came low and clear
6 The slow, sad, murmur of far distant seas. *imagery*
personification

7 Whipped by an icy breeze *imagery*
8 Upon a shore
9 Wind-swept and desolate.

10 It was a sunless strand that never bore
11 The footprints of a man,
12 Nor felt the weight *imagery*

13 Since time began
14 Of any human quality or stir,
15 Save what the dreary winds and wave incur.

16 And in the hush of waters was the sound
17 Of pebbles, rolling round; *personification*
18 For ever rolling, with a hollow sound: *imagery*

19 And, bubbling sea-weeds, as the waters go,
20 Swish to and fro *onomatopoeia, personification,*
21 Their long cold tentacles of slimy grey. *simile, imagery*

22 There was no day;
23 Nor ever came a night
24 Setting the stars alight

28

_{25 ℓ} To wonder at the moon: ~Sound, squeal~

_{26 ℓ} Was twilight only, and the (frightened) (croon,)

_{27 g} (Smitten) to (whimpers) of the (dreary wind) ~personification~ ~imagery~

_{28 g} And <u>waves</u> that <u>journeyed</u> (blind) ~Personification~

_{29 d} And then I <u>loosed my ear</u> ... O, it was sweet

_{30 f} To hear a cart go jolting down the street.

~imagery~

James Stephens (1882–1950)

The person put a shell to their ear heard an ocean, and imagined a beautiful beach scene. It was beautiful & sad because no one had ever stepped on that beach before. When the person moved the shell away from their ear, they were happy to hear a cart rolling down the street they were on.

~~Quatrain~~   Sonnet   ~~Couplet~~   Terset

Theme: Free verse

•Nature   Isolation

•Rememberance (person listening to shell & imagining the shell's home)

Very descriptive, puts an image of a beautiful beach in my head, as well as imagining the water as a person.

29

She Sells Seashells

She sells seashells by the seashore.
The shells that she sells are seashells, I'm sure.
So if she sells seashells by the seashore,
I'm sure that the shells are seashore shells.

Anon.

The Chambered Nautilus

This is the ship of pearl, which, poets feign,
    Sails the unshadowed main,—
      The venturous bark that flings
On the sweet summer wind its purpled wings
In gulfs enchanted, where the Siren sings,
    And coral reefs lie bare,
Where the cold sea-maids rise to sun their streaming
  hair.

Its webs of living gauze no more unfurl;
    Wrecked is the ship of pearl!
      And every chambered cell,
Where its dim dreaming life was wont to dwell,
As the frail tenant shaped his growing shell,
    Before thee lies revealed,—
Its irised ceiling rent, its sunless crypt unsealed!

Year after year beheld the silent toil
    That spread his lustrous coil;
      Still, as the spiral grew,
He left the past year's dwelling for the new,
Stole with soft step its shining archway through,
    Built up its idle door,
Stretched in his last-found home, and knew the old
  no more.

Thanks for the heavenly message brought by thee,
    Child of the wandering sea,
      Cast from her lap, forlorn!

From thy dead lips a clearer note is born
Than ever Triton blew from wreathèd horn!
     While on mine ear it rings,
Through the deep caves of thought I hear a voice that
    sings:—

Build thee more stately mansions, O my soul,
     As the swift seasons roll!
     Leave thy low-vaulted past!
Let each new temple, nobler than the last,
Shut thee from heaven with a dome more vast,
    Till thou at length art free,
Leaving thine outgrown shell by life's unresting sea!

Oliver Wendell Holmes (1809–1894)

By The Sea

Why does the sea moan evermore?
      Shut out from heaven it makes its moan,
It frets against the boundary shore;
      All earth's full rivers cannot fill
      The sea, that drinking thirsteth still.

Sheer miracles of loveliness
      Lie hid in its unlooked-on bed:
Anemones, salt, passionless,
      Blow flower-like; just enough alive
      To blow and multiply and thrive.

Shells quaint with curve, or spot, or spike,
      Encrusted live things argus-eyed,
All fair alike, yet all unlike,
      Are born without a pang, and die
      Without a pang, and so pass by.

Christina Rossetti (1830–1894)

Overheard on a Saltmarsh

A 1 Nymph, nymph, what are your beads?

B 2 Green glass, goblin. Why do you stare at them?

Alliteration
C 3 Give them me.

4 D No.

C 5 Give them me. Give them me.

6 D No.

7 A 6 Then I will howl all night in the reeds,
8 B 6 Lie in mud and howl for them.

9 D 8 Goblin, why do you love them so?

10 E 9 They are better than stars or water,
11 f 9 Better than voices of winds that sing, onomatopoeia
12 E 9 Better than any man's fair daughter,
13 f 9 Your green glass beads on a silver ring.

14 G Hush, I stole them out of the moon.

15 B Give me your beads, I want them.

16 D No.

34

G I will howl in a deep lagoon

D For your green glass beads, I love them so.

B Give them me. Give them.

Alliteration

D No.

Harold Monro (1879–1932)

Blank verse?

Theme: Selfishness

The Goblin wants the Nymph's green pearls, and will mourn if he doesn't get them.

The Goblin sees the Nymph's green beads. He asks for them & says he will whine if he doesn't get them. He tells the nymph that they are really pretty & would look good on jewelry. The nymph stole them at night. The goblin asks for the beads again & the nymph says "no".

Imagery

I like those lines because it shows how selfish people can be & what they would do to get what they want.

green - greed

green grass - better life / wealth

35

Seaweed

Seaweed sways and sways and swirls
as if swaying were its form of stillness;
and it flushes against fierce rock
it slips over it as shadows do, without hurting itself.

D. H. Lawrence (1885–1930)

Seaweed

When descends on the Atlantic
       The gigantic
Storm-wind of the equinox,
Landward in his wrath he scourges
       The toiling surges,
Laden with seaweed from the rocks:

From Bermuda's reefs; from edges
       Of sunken ledges,
In some far-off, bright Azore;
From Bahama, and the dashing,
       Silver-flashing
Surges of San Salvador;

From the tumbling surf, that buries
       The Orkneyan skerries,
Answering the hoarse Hebrides;
And from wrecks of ships, and drifting
       Spars, uplifting
On the desolate, rainy seas;—

Ever drifting, drifting, drifting
       On the shifting
Currents of the restless main;
Till in sheltered coves, and reaches
       Of sandy beaches,
All have found repose again.

So when storms of wild emotion
      Strike the ocean
Of the poet's soul, ere long
From each cave and rocky fastness,
      In its vastness,
Floats some fragment of a song:

From the far-off isles enchanted,
      Heaven has planted
With the golden fruit of Truth;
From the flashing surf, whose vision
      Gleams Elysian
In the tropic clime of Youth;

From the strong Will, and the Endeavor
      That for ever
Wrestle with the tides of Fate;
From the wreck of Hopes far-scattered,
      Tempest-shattered,
Floating waste and desolate;—

Ever drifting, drifting, drifting
      On the shifting
Currents of the restless heart;
Till at length in books recorded,
      They, like hoarded
Household words, no more depart.

Henry Wadsworth Longfellow (1807–1882)

I started early, took my dog

I started early, took my dog
And visited the sea
The mermaids in the basement
Came out to look at me

And frigates in the upper floor
Extended hempen hands
Presuming me to be a mouse
Aground, upon the sands

But no man moved me till the tide
Went past my simple shoe
And past my apron and my belt
And past my bodice too

And made as he would eat me up
As wholly as a dew
Upon a dandelion's sleeve
And then I started too

And he—he followed close behind
I felt his silver heel
Upon my ankle,—then my shoes
Would overflow with pearl

Until we met the solid town
No man he seemed to know
And bowing with a mighty look
At me, the sea withdrew

Emily Dickinson (1830–1886)

Strawberries and the Sailing Ship

We sat on the top of the cliff
Overlooking the open sea
Our backs turned to the little town
Each of us had a basket of strawberries
We had just bought them from a dark woman
With quick eyes – berry-finding eyes
They're fresh picked said she from our own garden
The tips of her fingers were stained a bright red!
Heavens what strawberries
Each one was the finest
The perfect berry – the strawberry Absolute
The fruit of our childhood!
The very air came fanning
On strawberry wings
And down below, in the pools
Little children were bathing
With strawberry wings
And down below, in the pools
Little children were bathing
With strawberry faces.
Over the blue swinging water
A three masted sailing ship
With nine ten eleven sails
Wonderfully beautifully!
She came riding
As though every sail were taking its fill
of the sun and the light.
And: Oh! how I'd love to be on board said Anne.
The captain was below, but the crew lay about

Idle and handsome –
Have some strawberries we said
Slipping and sliding on the polished decks
And shaking the baskets

Katherine Mansfield (1888–1923)

The Sea-Shore

I should like to dwell where the deep blue sea
Rock'd to and fro as tranquilly,
As if it were willing the halcyon's nest
Should shelter through summer its beautiful guest.
When a plaining murmur like that of a song.
And a silvery line come the waves along:
Now bathing – now leaving the gentle shore.
Where shining sea-shells lay scattered o'er.
And children wandering along the strand.
With the eager eye and the busy hand,
Heaping the pebbles and green sea-weed,
Like treasures laid up for a time of need.
Or tempting the waves with their daring feet.
To launch, perhaps, some tiny fleet:
Mimicking those which bear afar
The wealth of trade – and the strength of war.
I should love, when the sun-set reddened the foam,
To watch the fisherman's boat come home,
With his well-filled net and glittering spoil:
Well has the noon-tide repaid its toil.
While the ships that lie in the distance away
Catch on their canvass the crimsoning ray:
Like fairy ships in the tales of old,
When the sails they spread were purple and gold.
Then the deep delight of the starry night.
With its shadowy depths and dreamy light:
When far away spreads the boundless sea,
As if it imagined infinity

Let me hear the winds go singing by,
Lulling the waves with their melody:
While the moon like a mother watches their sleep,
And I ask no home but beside the deep.

Letitia Elizabeth Landon (1802–1838)

Seaside

Swiftly out from the friendly lilt of the band,
    The crowd's good laughter, the loved eyes of men,
    I am drawn nightward; I must turn again
Where, down beyond the low untrodden strand,
There curves and glimmers outward to the unknown
    The old unquiet ocean. All the shade
Is rife with magic and movement. I stray alone
    Here on the edge of silence, half afraid,

Waiting a sign. In the deep heart of me
The sullen waters swell towards the moon,
And all my tides set seaward.
                  From inland
Leaps a gay fragment of some mocking tune,
That tinkles and laughs and fades along the sand,
And dies between the seawall and the sea.

Rupert Brooke (1887–1915)

At the Sea-Side

When I was down beside the sea
A wooden spade they gave to me
To dig the sandy shore.

My holes were empty like a cup.
In every hole the sea came up,
Till it could come no more.

Robert Louis Stevenson (1850–1894)

And if I did, what then?

'And if I did, what then?
          Are you aggrieved therefore?
The sea hath fish for every man,
          And what would you have more?'

Thus did my mistress once
          Amaze my mind with doubt;
And popped a question for the nonce,
          To beat my brains about.

Whereto I thus replied:
          'Each fisherman can wish
That all the seas at every tide
          Were his alone to fish.

'And so did I, in vain:
          But since it may not be,
Let such fish there as find the gain,
          And leave the loss for me.

'And with such luck and loss
          I will content myself,
Till tides of turning time may toss
          Such fishers on the shelf.

'And when they stick on sands,
          That every man may see,
Then will I laugh and clap my hands,
          As they do now at me.'

George Gascoigne (c. 1535–1577)

Dover Beach

The sea is calm tonight.
The tide is full, the moon lies fair
Upon the straits; on the French coast the light
Gleams and is gone; the cliffs of England stand,
Glimmering and vast, out in the tranquil bay.
Come to the window, sweet is the night-air!
Only, from the long line of spray
Where the sea meets the moon-blanched land,
Listen! you hear the grating roar
Of pebbles which the waves draw back, and fling,
At their return, up the high strand,
Begin, and cease, and then again begin,
With tremulous cadence slow, and bring
The eternal note of sadness in.

Sophocles long ago
Heard it on the Ægean, and it brought
Into his mind the turbid ebb and flow
Of human misery; we
Find also in the sound a thought,
Hearing it by this distant northern sea.

The Sea of Faith
Was once, too, at the full, and round earth's shore
Lay like the folds of a bright girdle furled.
But now I only hear
Its melancholy, long, withdrawing roar,
Retreating, to the breath
Of the night-wind, down the vast edges drear
And naked shingles of the world.

Ah, love, let us be true
To one another! for the world, which seems
To lie before us like a land of dreams,
So various, so beautiful, so new,
Hath really neither joy, nor love, nor light,
Nor certitude, nor peace, nor help for pain;
And we are here as on a darkling plain
Swept with confused alarms of struggle and flight,
Where ignorant armies clash by night.

Matthew Arnold (1822–1888)

Meeting at Night

I

The grey sea and the long black land;
And the yellow half-moon large and low;
And the startled little waves that leap
In fiery ringlets from their sleep,
As I gain the cove with pushing prow,
And quench its speed i' the slushy sand.

II

Then a mile of warm sea-scented beach;
Three fields to cross till a farm appears;
A tap at the pane, the quick sharp scratch
And blue spurt of a lighted match,
And a voice less loud, thro' its joys and fears,
Than the two hearts beating each to each!

Robert Browning (1812–1889)

Amoretti LXXV: One Day I Wrote her Name

One day I wrote her name upon the strand,
But came the waves and washed it away:
Again I wrote it with a second hand,
But came the tide, and made my pains his prey.
"Vain man," said she, "that dost in vain assay,
A mortal thing so to immortalize;
For I myself shall like to this decay,
And eke my name be wiped out likewise."
"Not so," (quod I) "let baser things devise
To die in dust, but you shall live by fame:
My verse your vertues rare shall eternize,
And in the heavens write your glorious name:
Where whenas death shall all the world subdue,
Our love shall live, and later life renew."

Edmund Spenser (c.1552–1599)

Come unto these Yellow Sands

from The Tempest

Come unto these yellow sands,
    And then take hands:
Court'sied when you have, and kissed,
    The wild waves whist, –
Foot it featly here and there;
And, sweet sprites, the burden bear.
    Hark, hark!
        Bow, wow,
    The watch-dogs bark:
        Bow, wow.
    Hark, hark! I hear
The strain of strutting chanticleer
Cry, Cock-a-diddle-dow!

William Shakespeare (1564–1616)

Like as the waves make towards
the pebbled shore

Sonnet LX

Like as the waves make towards the pebbled shore,
So do our minutes hasten to their end;
Each changing place with that which goes before,
In sequent toil all forwards do contend.
Nativity, once in the main of light,
Crawls to maturity, where with being crowned,
Crooked eclipses 'gainst his glory fight,
And Time that gave doth now his gift confound.
Time doth transfix the flourish set on youth
And delves the parallels in beauty's brow,
Feeds on the rarities of nature's truth,
And nothing stands but for his scythe to mow:
    And yet to times in hope for my verse shall stand,
    Praising thy worth, despite his cruel hand.

William Shakespeare (1564–1616)

Beeny Cliff

I

O the opal and the sapphire of that wandering
   western sea,
And the woman riding high above with bright hair
   flapping free –
The woman whom I loved so, and who loyally loved
   me.

II

The pale mews plained below us, and the waves
   seemed far away
In a nether sky, engrossed in saying their ceaseless
   babbling say,
As we laughed light-heartedly aloft on that clear-
   sunned March day.

III

A little cloud then cloaked us, and there flew an irised
   rain,
And the Atlantic dyed its levels with a dull
   misfeatured stain,
And then the sun burst out again, and purples
   prinked the main.

IV

– Still in all its chasmal beauty bulks old Beeny to the
    sky,
And shall she and I not go there once again now
    March is nigh,
And the sweet things said in that March say anew
    there by and by?

V

What if still in chasmal beauty looms that wild weird
    western shore,
The woman now is – elsewhere – whom the ambling
    pony bore,
And nor knows nor cares for Beeny, and will laugh
    there
        nevermore.

Thomas Hardy (1840–1928)

Parting at Morning

Round the cape of a sudden came the sea,
And the sun looked over the mountain's rim:
And straight was a path of gold for him,
And the need of a world of men for me.

Robert Browning (1812–1889)

O CAPTAIN! MY CAPTAIN!:
CAPTAINS AND SAILORS

rhyme - iambic

about Abraham Lincoln

In death there is a lot of sorrow, but
there is also joy.

There is loss in victory.
~~Price of victory~~can come at a high price.
free verse - meter

Elegy - type of poem

~~Anaphora~~

Symbolism - Captain = Abraham Lincoln
    metaphor

Ship - ~~slavery~~
Prize - abolishion of slavery

O Captain! My Captain!

Refrain

1 O Captain! my Captain! our fearful trip is done;

2 The ship has weather'd every rack, the prize we
sought is won;

3 The port is near, the bells I hear, the people all
exulting,

4 While follow eyes the steady keel, the vessel grim and
daring:

5 But O heart! heart! heart!

6 O the bleeding drops of red,

7 Where on the deck my Captain lies,

8 Fallen cold and dead.

refrain

9 O Captain! my Captain! rise up and hear the bells;

10 Rise up – for you the flag is flung – for you the bugle
trills;

11 For you bouquets and ribbon'd wreaths – for you the
shores a-crowding;

12 For you they call, the swaying mass, their eager faces
turning;

13 Here Captain! dear father!

14 This arm beneath your head;

15 It is some dream that on the deck,

16 You've fallen cold and dead.

engagement

> Tells the reader the captain is
> dead before it's announced.
> Descriptive & puts an image
> in my mind.
> I like the way it was
> written.

foreshadowing

59

My Captain does not answer, his lips are pale and
   still;
My father does not feel my arm, he has no pulse nor
   will;
The ship is anchor'd safe and sound, its voyage closed
   and done;
From fearful trip the victor ship comes in with object
   won;
      Exult O shores, and ring O bells!
        But I with mournful tread,
          Walk the deck my Captain lies,
            Fallen cold and dead.

Walt Whitman (1819–1892)

from Elegy on Captain Cook

Say first, what Power inspir'd his dauntless breast
With scorn of danger, and inglorious rest,
To quit imperial London's gorgeous domes,
Where, deck'd in thousand tints, bright Pleasure roams;
In cups of summer-ice her nectar pours,
Or twines, 'mid wint'ry snows, her roseate bowers . . .
Where Beauty moves with fascinating grace,
Calls the sweet blush to wanton o'er her face,
On each fond youth her soft artillery tries,
Aims her light smile, and rolls her frolic eyes:
What Power inspir'd his dauntless breast to brave
The scorch'd Equator, and th'Antarctic wave?

Anna Seward (1742–1809)

The Sailor Boy

He rose at dawn and, fired with hope,
Shot o'er the seething harbour-bar,
And reach'd the ship and caught the rope,
And whistled to the morning star.

And while he whistled long and loud
He heard a fierce mermaiden cry,
"O boy, tho' thou are young and proud,
I see the place where thou wilt lie.

"The sands and yeasty surges mix
In caves about the dreary bay,
And on thy ribs the limpet sticks,
And in thy heart the scrawl shall play."

"Fool," he answer'd , "death is sure
To those that stay and those that roam,
But I will nevermore endure
To sit with empty hands at home.

"My mother clings about my neck,
My sisters crying, 'Stay for shame;'
My father raves of death and wreck, –
They are all to blame, they are all to blame.

"God help me! save I take my part
Of danger on the roaring sea,
A devil rises in my heart,
Far worse than any death to me."

Alfred, Lord Tennyson (1809–1892)

Casabianca

The boy stood on the burning deck,
    Whence all but him had fled;
The flame that lit the battle's wreck,
    Shone round him o'er the dead.
Yet beautiful and bright he stood,
    As born to rule the storm;
A creature of heroic blood,
    A proud, though childlike form.

The flames rolled on; he would not go
    Without his father's word;
That father, faint in death below,
    His voice no longer heard.

He called aloud – "Say, father, say
    If yet my task is done?"
He knew not that the chieftain lay
    Unconscious of his son.

"Speak, father!" once again he cried,
    "If I may yet be gone!"
And but the booming shots replied,
    And fast the flames rolled on.

Upon his brow he felt their breath,
    And in his waving hair;
And looked from that lone post of death
    In still yet brave despair;

And shouted but once more aloud,
  "My father! must I stay?"
While o'er him fast, through sail and shroud,
  The wreathing fires made way.

They wrapped the ship in splendour wild,
  They caught the flag on high,
And streamed above the gallant child,
  Like banners in the sky.

There came a burst of thunder sound;
  The boy – Oh! where was *he*?
Ask of the winds that far around
  With fragments strewed the sea, –

With mast, and helm, and pennon fair,
  That well had borne their part, –
But the noblest thing which perished there,
  Was that young, faithful heart.

Felicia Hemans (1793–1835)

Sir Humphrey Gilbert

Southward with fleet of ice
    Sailed the corsair Death;
Wild and fast blew the blast,
    And the east-wind was his breath.

His lordly ships of ice
    Glisten in the sun;
On each side, like pennons wide,
    Flashing crystal streamlets run.

His sails of white sea-mist
    Dripped with silver rain;
But where he passed there were cast
    Leaden shadows o'er the main.

Eastward from Campobello
    Sir Humphrey Gilbert sailed;
Three days or more seaward he bore,
    Then, alas! the land-wind failed.

Alas! the land-wind failed,
    And ice-cold grew the night;
And nevermore, on sea or shore,
    Should Sir Humphrey see the light.

He sat upon the deck,
    The Book was in his hand;
"Do not fear! Heaven is as near,"
    He said, "by water as by land!"

In the first watch of the night,
        Without a signal's sound,
Out of the sea, mysteriously,
        The fleet of Death rose all around.

The moon and the evening star
        Were hanging in the shrouds;
Every mast, as it passed,
        Seemed to rake the passing clouds.

They grappled with their prize,
        At midnight black and cold!
As of a rock was the shock;
        Heavily the ground-swell rolled.

Southward through day and dark,
        They drift in close embrace,
With mist and rain, o'er the open main;
        Yet there seems no change of place.

Southward, forever southward,
        They drift through dark and day;
And like a dream, in the Gulf-Stream
        Sinking, vanish all away.

Henry Wadsworth Longfellow (1807–1882)

My Bounding Bark

My bounding bark, I fly to thee, –
    I'm wearied of the shore;
I long to hail the swelling sea,
    And wander free once more:
A sailor's life of reckless glee,
    That only is the life for me!

I was born not for fashion's slave,
    Or the dull city strife;
Be mine the spirit-stirring wave,
    The roving sailor's life:
A life of freedom on the sea,
    That only is the life for me!

I was not born for lighted halls,
    Or the gay revel's round;
My music is where Ocean calls,
    And echoing rocks resound:
The wandering sailor's life of glee,
    That only is the life for me!

Anon.

Drunken Sailor

What shall we do with a drunken sailor,
What shall we do with a drunken sailor,
What shall we do with a drunken sailor,
      Early in the morning?
   Way-aye, there she rises,
   Way-aye, there she rises,
   Way-aye, there she rises,
      Early in the morning!

Chuck him in the long-boat till he gets sober,
Chuck him in the long-boat till he gets sober,
Chuck him in the long-boat till he gets sober,
      Early in the morning!
   Way-aye, there she rises,
   Way-aye, there she rises,
   Way-aye, there she rises,
      Early in the morning!

Anon.

from The Rime of the Ancient Mariner

PART I

It is an ancient Mariner,
And he stoppeth one of three.
'By thy long grey beard and glittering eye,
Now wherefore stopp'st thou me?

The Bridegroom's doors are opened wide,
And I am next of kin;
The guests are met, the feast is set:
May'st hear the merry din.'

He holds him with his skinny hand,
'There was a ship,' quoth he.
'Hold off! unhand me, grey-beard loon!'
Eftsoons his hand dropt he.

He holds him with his glittering eye—
The Wedding-Guest stood still,
And listens like a three years' child:
The Mariner hath his will.

The Wedding-Guest sat on a stone:
He cannot choose but hear;
And thus spake on that ancient man,
The bright-eyed Mariner.

'The ship was cheered, the harbour cleared,
Merrily did we drop
Below the kirk, below the hill,
Below the lighthouse top.

The Sun came up upon the left,
Out of the sea came he!
And he shone bright, and on the right
Went down into the sea.

Higher and higher every day,
Till over the mast at noon—'
The Wedding-Guest here beat his breast,
For he heard the loud bassoon.

The bride hath paced into the hall,
Red as a rose is she;
Nodding their heads before her goes
The merry minstrelsy.

The Wedding-Guest he beat his breast,
Yet he cannot choose but hear;
And thus spake on that ancient man,
The bright-eyed Mariner.

And now the STORM-BLAST came, and he
Was tyrannous and strong:
He struck with his o'ertaking wings,
And chased us south along.

With sloping masts and dipping prow,
As who pursued with yell and blow
Still treads the shadow of his foe,
And forward bends his head,
The ship drove fast, loud roared the blast,
And southward aye we fled.

And now there came both mist and snow,
And it grew wondrous cold:
And ice, mast-high, came floating by,
As green as emerald.

And through the drifts the snowy clifts
Did send a dismal sheen:
Nor shapes of men nor beasts we ken—
The ice was all between.

The ice was here, the ice was there,
The ice was all around:
It cracked and growled, and roared and howled,
Like noises in a swound!

At length did cross an Albatross,
Thorough the fog it came;
As if it had been a Christian soul,
We hailed it in God's name.

It ate the food it ne'er had eat,
And round and round it flew.
The ice did split with a thunder-fit;
The helmsman steered us through!

And a good south wind sprung up behind;
The Albatross did follow,
And every day, for food or play,
Came to the mariner's hollo!

In mist or cloud, on mast or shroud,
It perched for vespers nine;
Whiles all the night, through fog-smoke white,
Glimmered the white Moon-shine.'

'God save thee, ancient Mariner!
From the fiends, that plague thee thus!—
Why look'st thou so?'—With my cross-bow
I shot the ALBATROSS.

PART II

The Sun now rose upon the right:
Out of the sea came he,
Still hid in mist, and on the left
Went down into the sea.

And the good south wind still blew behind,
But no sweet bird did follow,
Nor any day for food or play
Came to the mariner's hollo!

And I had done a hellish thing,
And it would work 'em woe:
For all averred, I had killed the bird
That made the breeze to blow.
Ah wretch! said they, the bird to slay,
That made the breeze to blow!

Nor dim nor red, like God's own head,
The glorious Sun uprist:
Then all averred, I had killed the bird
That brought the fog and mist.

'Twas right, said they, such birds to slay,
That bring the fog and mist.
The fair breeze blew, the white foam flew,

The furrow followed free;
We were the first that ever burst
Into that silent sea.

Down dropt the breeze, the sails dropt down,
'Twas sad as sad could be;
And we did speak only to break
The silence of the sea!

All in a hot and copper sky,
The bloody Sun, at noon,
Right up above the mast did stand,
No bigger than the Moon.

Day after day, day after day,
We stuck, nor breath nor motion;
As idle as a painted ship
Upon a painted ocean.

Water, water, every where,
And all the boards did shrink;
Water, water, every where,
Nor any drop to drink.

The very deep did rot: O Christ!
That ever this should be!
Yea, slimy things did crawl with legs
Upon the slimy sea.

About, about, in reel and rout
The death-fires danced at night;
The water, like a witch's oils,
Burnt green, and blue and white.

And some in dreams assurèd were
Of the Spirit that plagued us so;
Nine fathom deep he had followed us
From the land of mist and snow.

And every tongue, through utter drought,
Was withered at the root;
We could not speak, no more than if
We had been choked with soot.

Ah! well a-day! what evil looks
Had I from old and young!
Instead of the cross, the Albatross
About my neck was hung.

Samuel Taylor Coleridge (1772–1834)

The Castaway

Obscurest night involved the sky,
    The Atlantic billows roared,
When such a destined wretch as I,
    Washed headlong from on board,
Of friends, of hope, of all bereft,
His floating home for ever left.

No braver chief could Albion boast
    Than he with whom he went,
Nor ever ship left Albion's coast
    With warmer wishes sent.
He loved them both, but both in vain,
Nor him behold, nor her again.

Not long beneath the whelming brine,
    Expert to swim, he lay;
Nor soon he felt his strength decline,
    Or courage die away;
But waged with death a lasting strife,
Supported by despair of life.

He shouted: not his friends had failed
    To check his vessel's course,
But so the furious blast prevailed
    That, pitiless perforce,
They left their outcast mate behind,
And scudded still before the wind.

Some succour yet they could afford;
    And such as storms allow,
The cask, the coop, the floated cord,
    Delayed not to bestow.
But he (they knew) nor ship not shore,
Whate'er they gave, should visit more.

Not, cruel as it seemed, could he
    Their haste himself condemn,
Aware that flight, in such a sea,
    Alone could rescue them;
Yet bitter felt it still to die
Deserted, and his friends so nigh.

He long survives, who lives an hour
    In ocean, self-upheld;
And so long he, with unspent power,
    His destiny repelled;
And ever, as the minutes flew,
Entreated help, or cried 'Adieu!'

At length, his transient respite past,
    His comrades, who before
Had heard his voice in every blast,
    Could catch the sound no more:
For then, by toil subdued, he drank
The stifling wave, and then he sank.

No poet wept him; but the page
    Of narrative sincere,
That tells his name, his worth, his age,
    Is wet with Anson's tear:
And tears by bards or heroes shed
Alike immortalise the dead.

I therefore purpose not, or dream,
　　Descanting on his fate,
To give the melancholy theme
　　A more enduring date:
But misery still delights to trace
Its semblance in another's case.

No voice divine the storm allayed,
　　No light propitious shone,
When, snatched from all effectual aid,
　　We perished, each alone:
But I beneath a rougher sea,
And whelmed in deeper gulfs than he.

William Cowper (1731–1800)

I WAS BORN UPON THY BANK:
RIVERS

I Was Born Upon Thy Bank, River

I was born upon thy bank, river,
    My blood flows in thy stream,
And thou meanderest forever
    At the bottom of my dream.

Henry David Thoreau (1817–1862)

The River

I came from the sunny valleys
And sought for the open sea,
For I thought in its gray expanses
My peace would come to me.

I came at last to the ocean
And found it wild and black,
And I cried to the windless valleys,
"Be kind and take me back!"

But the thirsty tide ran inland,
And the salt waves drank of me,
And I who was fresh as the rainfall
Am bitter as the sea.

Sara Teasdale (1884–1933)

Afton Water

Flow gently, sweet Afton, among thy green braes,
Flow gently, I'll sing thee a song in thy praise;
My Mary's asleep by thy murmuring stream,
Flow gently, sweet Afton, disturb not her dream.

Thou stock-dove, whose echo resounds thro' the glen,
Ye wild whistling blackbirds in yon thorny den,
Thou green-crested lapwing, thy screaming forbear,
I charge you disturb not my slumbering fair.

How lofty, sweet Afton, thy neighbouring hills,
Far mark'd with the courses of clear winding rills;
There daily I wander as noon rises high,
My flocks and my Mary's sweet cot in my eye.

How pleasant thy banks and green valleys below,
Where wild in the woodlands the primroses blow;
There oft, as mild Ev'ning sweeps over the lea,
The sweet-scented birk shades my Mary and me.

Thy crystal stream, Afton, how lovely it glides,
And winds by the cot where my Mary resides,
How wanton thy waters her snowy feet lave,
As gathering sweet flowrets she stems thy clear wave.

Flow gently, sweet Afton, among thy green braes,
Flow gently, sweet river, the theme of my lays;
My Mary's asleep by thy murmuring stream,
Flow gently, sweet Afton, disturb not her dream.

Robert Burns (1759–1796)

By Severn

If England, her spirit lives anywhere
It is by Severn, by hawthorns, and grand willows.
Earth heaves up twice a hundred feet in air
And ruddy clay falls scooped out to the weedy
    shallows.
There in the brakes of May Spring has her chambers,
Robing-rooms of hawthorn, cowslip, cuckoo flower –
Wonder complete changes for each square joy's hour,
Past thought miracles are there and beyond numbers.
If for the drab atmospheres and managed lighting
In London town, Oriana's playwrights had
Wainlode her theatre and then coppice clad
Hill for her ground of sauntering and idle waiting.
Why, then I think, our chieftest glory of pride
(The Elizabethans of Thames, South and Northern
    side)
Would nothing of its needing be denied,
And her sons praises from England's mouth again be
    outcried.

Ivor Gurney (1890–1937)

To the River Charles

River! that in silence windest
Through the meadows, bright and free,
Till at length thy rest thou findest
In the bosom of the sea!
Four long years of mingled feeling,
Half in rest, and half in strife,
I have seen thy waters stealing
Onward, like the stream of life.
Thou hast taught me, Silent River!
Many a lesson, deep and long;
Thou hast been a generous giver;
I can give thee but a song.
Oft in sadness and in illness,
I have watched thy current glide,
Till the beauty of its stillness
Overflowed me, like a tide.
And in better hours and brighter,
When I saw thy waters gleam,
I have felt my heart beat lighter,
And leap onward with thy stream.
Not for this alone I love thee,
Nor because thy waves of blue
From celestial seas above thee
Take their own celestial hue.
Where yon shadowy woodlands hide thee,
And thy waters disappear,
Friends I love have dwelt beside thee,
And have made thy margin dear.
More than this;—thy name reminds me
Of three friends, all true and tried;
And that name, like magic, binds me

Closer, closer to thy side.
Friends my soul with joy remembers!
How like quivering flames they start,
When I fan the living embers
On the hearth-stone of my heart!
'T is for this, thou Silent River!
That my spirit leans to thee;
Thou hast been a generous giver,
Take this idle song from me.

Henry Wadsworth Longfellow (1807–1882)

Ouse

Here Ouse, slow winding through a level plain
Of spacious meads with cattle sprinkled o'er,
Conducts the eye along its sinuous course
Delighted. There, fast rooted in their bank,
Stand, never overlook'd, our fav'rite elms,
That screen the herdman's solitary hut;
While far beyond, and overthwart the stream
That, as with molten glass, inlays the vale,
The sloping land recedes into the clouds;
Displaying on its varied side the grace
Of hedge-row beauties numberless, square tow'r
Tall spire, from which the sound of cheerful bells
Just undulates upon the list'ning ear,
Groves, heaths, and smoking villages, remote.

William Cowper (1731–1800)

The Fens

There's not a hill in all the view,
Save that a forkèd cloud or two
Upon the verge of distance lies
And into mountains cheats the eyes.
And as to trees the willows wear
Lopped heads as high as bushes are;
Some taller things the distance shrouds
That may be trees or stacks or clouds
Or may be nothing; still they wear
A semblance where there's nought to spare.

Among the tawny tasselled reed
The ducks and ducklings float and feed.
With head oft dabbing in the flood
They fish all day the weedy mud,
And tumbler-like are bobbing there,
Heels topsy turvy in the air.

The geese in troops come droving up,
Nibble the weeds, and take a sup;
And, closely puzzled to agree,
Chatter like gossips over tea.
The gander with his scarlet nose
When strife's at height will interpose,
And, stretching neck to that and this,
With now a mutter, now a hiss,
A nibble at the feathers too,
A sort of 'pray be quiet do,'
And turning as the matter mends,
He stills them into mutual friends;
Then in a sort of triumph sings

And throws the water o'er his wings.
Ah, could I see a spinney nigh,
A puddock riding in the sky
Above the oaks with easy sail
On stilly wings and forked tail,
Or meet a heath of furze in flower,
I might enjoy a quiet hour,
Sit down at rest, and walk at ease,
And find a many things to please.
But here my fancy's moods admire
The naked levels till they tire,
Nor e'en a molehill cushion meet
To rest on when I want a seat.
Here's little save the river scene
And grounds of oats in rustling green
And crowded growth of wheat and beans,
That with the hope of plenty leans
And cheers the farmer's gazing brow,
Who lives and triumphs in the plough –
One sometimes meets a pleasant sward
Of swarthy grass; and quickly marred
The plough soon turns it into brown,
And, when again one rambles down
The path, small hillocks burning lie
And smoke beneath a burning sky.
Green paddocks have but little charms
With gain the merchandise of farms;
And, muse and marvel where we may,
Gain mars the landscape every day –
The meadow grass turned up and copt,
The trees to stumpy dotterels lopt,
The hearth with fuel to supply
For rest to smoke and chatter bye;
Giving the joy of home delights,

The warmest mirth on coldest nights.
And so for gain, that joy's repay,
Change cheats the landscape every day,
Nor trees nor bush about it grows
That from the hatchet can repose,
And the horizon stooping smiles
Oer treeless fens of many miles.
Spring comes and goes and comes again
And all is nakedness and fen.

John Clare (1793–1864)

The River

With ceaseless motion comes and goes the tide,
Flowing, it fills the channel vast and wide;
Then back to sea, with strong majestic sweep
It rolls, in ebb yet terrible and deep;
Here samphire-banks and salt-wort bound the flood,
There stakes and sea-weeds withering on the mud;
And higher up, a ridge of all things base,
Which some strong tide has rolled upon the place.
     Thy gentle river boasts its pygmy boat,
Urged on by pains, half grounded, half afloat;
While at her stern an angler takes his stand,
And marks the fish he purposes to land
From that clear space, where, in the cheerful ray
Of the warm sun, the sealy people play.
     Far other craft our prouder river shows,
Hoys, pinks, and sloops; brigs, brigantines, and snows:
Nor angler we on our wide stream descry,
But one poor dredger where his oysters lie:
He, cold and wet, and driving with the tide,
Beats his weak arms against his tarry side,
Then drains the remnant of diluted gin,
To aid the warmth that languishes within;
Renewing oft his poor attempts to beat
His tangling fingers into gathering heat.

George Crabbe (1754–1832)

The River-God's Song

Do not fear to put thy feet
Naked in the river sweet;
Think not leech or newt or toad
Will bite thy foot when thou hast trod;
Nor let the water rising high
As thou wad'st in make thee cry
And sob, but ever live with me,
And not a wave shall trouble thee.

John Fletcher (1579–1625)

Sonnets from The River Duddon:
After-Thought

I thought of Thee, my partner and my guide,
As being past away. – Vain sympathies!
For, backward, Duddon! as I cast my eyes,
I see what was, and is, and will abide;
Still glides the Stream, and shall for ever glide;
The Form remains, the Function never dies;
While we, the brave, the mighty, and the wise,
We Men, who in our morn of youth defied
The elements, must vanish; – be it so!
Enough, if something from our hands have power
To live, and act, and serve the future hour;
And if, as toward the silent tomb we go,
Through love, through hope, and faith's transcendent
  dower,
We feel that we are greater than we know.

William Wordsworth (1770–1850)

The Green River

I know a green grass path that leaves the field,
And like a running river, winds along
Into a leafy wood where is no throng
Of birds at noon-day, and no soft throats yield
Their music to the moon. The place is sealed,
An unclaimed sovereignty of voiceless song,
And all the unravished silences belong
To some sweet singer lost or unrevealed.
So is my soul become a silent place.
Oh, may I wake from this uneasy night
To find a voice of music manifold.
Let it be shape of sorrow with wan face,
Or Love that swoons on sleep, or else delight
That is as wide-eyed as a marigold.

Lord Alfred Douglas (1870–1945)

Prothalamion

Calm was the day, and through the trembling air
Sweet breathing Zephyrus did softly play,
A gentle spirit, that lightly did delay
Hot Titan's beams, which then did glister fair;
When I whose sullen care,
Through discontent of my long fruitless stay
In prince's court, and expectation vain
Of idle hopes, which still do fly away
Like empty shadows, did afflict my brain,
Walked forth to ease my pain
Along the shore of silver streaming Thames,
Whose rutty bank, the which his river hems,
Was painted all with variable flowers,
And all the meads adorned with dainty gems,
Fit to deck maidens' bowers,
And crown their paramours,
Against the bridal day, which is not long:
　　Sweet Thames, run softly, till I end my song.

There, in a meadow, by the river's side,
A flock of nymphs I chanced to espy,
All lovely daughters of the flood thereby,
With goodly greenish locks, all loose untied,
As each had been a bride;
And each one had a little wicker basket,
Made of fine twigs, entrailed curiously,
In which they gathered flowers to fill their flasket,
And with fine fingers cropt full featously
The tender stalks on high.
Of every sort, which in that meadow grew,
They gathered some; the violet pallid blue,

The little daisy, that at evening closes,
The virgin lily, and the primrose true,
With store of vermeil roses,
To deck their bridegrooms' posies
Against the bridal day, which was not long:
   Sweet Thames, run softly, till I end my song.

With that, I saw two swans of goodly hue
Come softly swimming down along the Lee;
Two fairer birds I yet did never see.
The snow which doth the top of Pindus strew,
Did never whiter shew,
Nor Jove himself, when he a swan would be
For love of Leda, whiter did appear:
Yet Leda was they say as white as he,
Yet not so white as these, nor nothing near.
So purely white they were,
That even the gentle stream, the which them bare,
Seemed foul to them, and bade his billows spare
To wet their silken feathers, lest they might
Soil their fair plumes with water not so fair,
And mar their beauties bright,
That shone as heaven's light,
Against their bridal day, which was not long:
   Sweet Thames, run softly, till I end my song.

Eftsoons the nymphs, which now had flowers their fill,
Ran all in haste, to see that silver brood,
As they came floating on the crystal flood.
Whom when they saw, they stood amazed still,
Their wondering eyes to fill.
Them seemed they never saw a sight so fair,
Of fowls so lovely, that they sure did deem
Them heavenly born, or to be that same pair

Which through the sky draw Venus' silver team;
For sure they did not seem
To be begot of any earthly seed,
But rather angels, or of angels' breed:
Yet were they bred of Somers-heat they say,
In sweetest season, when each flower and weed
The earth did fresh array,
So fresh they seemed as day,
Even as their bridal day, which was not long:
    Sweet Thames, run softly, till I end my song.

Then forth they all out of their baskets drew
Great store of flowers, the honour of the field,
That to the sense did fragrant odours yield,
All which upon those goodly birds they threw,
And all the waves did strew,
That like old Peneus' waters they did seem,
When down along by pleasant Tempe's shore,
Scattered with flowers, through Thessaly they stream,
That they appear through lilies' plenteous store,
Like a bride's chamber floor.
Two of those nymphs meanwhile, two garlands
    bound,
Of freshest flowers which in that mead they found,
The which presenting all in trim array,
Their snowy foreheads therewithal they crowned,
Whilst one did sing this lay,
Prepared against that day,
Against their bridal day, which was not long:
    Sweet Thames, run softly, till I end my song.

'Ye gentle birds, the world's fair ornament,
And heaven's glory, whom this happy hour
Doth lead unto your lovers' blissful bower,

Joy may you have and gentle heart's content
Of your love's complement:
And let fair Venus, that is queen of love,
With her heart-quelling son upon you smile,
Whose smile, they say, hath virtue to remove
All love's dislike, and friendship's faulty guile
For ever to assoil.
Let endless peace your steadfast hearts accord,
And blessed plenty wait upon your board,
And let your bed with pleasures chaste abound,
That fruitful issue may to you afford,
Which may your foes confound,
And make your joys redound
Upon your bridal day, which is not long:
　　Sweet Thames, run softly, till I end my song.'

So ended she; and all the rest around
To her redoubled that her undersong,
Which said their bridal day should not be long.
And gentle echo from the neighbour ground
Their accents did resound.
So forth those joyous birds did pass along,
Adown the Lee, that to them murmured low,
As he would speak, but that he lacked a tongue,
Yet did by signs his glad affection show,
Making his stream run slow.
And all the fowl which in his flood did dwell
Gan flock about these twain, that did excel
The rest so far as Cynthia doth shend
The lesser stars. So they, enranged well,
Did on those two attend,
And their best service lend,
Against their wedding day, which was not long:
　　Sweet Thames, run softly, till I end my song.

98

At length they all to merry London came,
To merry London, my most kindly nurse,
That to me gave this life's first native source;
Though from another place I take my name,
An house of ancient fame.
There when they came, whereas those bricky towers,
The which on Thames' broad aged back do ride,
Where now the studious lawyers have their bowers
There whilom wont the Templar Knights to bide,
Till they decayed through pride:
Next whereunto there stands a stately place,
Where oft I gained gifts and goodly grace
Of that great lord, which therein wont to dwell,
Whose want too well now feels my friendless case.
But ah, here fits not well
Old woes but joys to tell
Against the bridal day, which is not long:
   Sweet Thames, run softly, till I end my song.

Yet therein now doth lodge a noble peer,
Great England's glory, and the world's wide wonder,
Whose dreadful name late through all Spain did
   thunder,
And Hercules' two pillars standing near
Did make to quake and fear:
Fair branch of honour, flower of chivalry,
That fillest England with thy triumph's fame,
Joy have thou of thy noble victory,
And endless happiness of thine own name
That promiseth the same:
That through thy prowess and victorious arms,
Thy country may be freed from foreign harms;
And great Elisa's glorious name may ring
Through all the world, filled with thy wide alarms,

Which some brave Muse may sing
To ages following,
Upon the bridal day, which is not long:
   Sweet Thames, run softly, till I end my song.

From those high towers this noble lord issuing,
Like radiant Hesper when his golden hair
In th'Ocean billows he hath bathed fair,
Descended to the river's open viewing,
With a great train ensuing.
Above the rest were goodly to be seen
Two gentle knights of lovely face and feature
Beseeming well the bower of any queen,
With gifts of wit and ornaments of nature,
Fit for so goodly stature;
That like the twins of Jove they seemed in sight,
Which deck the baldric of the heavens bright.
They two forth pacing to the river's side,
Received those two fair birds, their love's delight;
Which, at th' appointed tide,
Each one did make his bride
Against their bridal day, which is not long:
Sweet Thames, run softly, till I end my song.

Edmund Spenser (c.1552–1599)

Looking Glass River

Smooth it glides upon its travel,
       Here a wimple, there a gleam—
O the clean gravel!
       O the smooth stream!

Sailing blossoms, silver fishes,
       Pave pools as clear as air—
How a child wishes
       To live down there!

We can see our colored faces
       Floating on the shaken pool
Down in cool places,
       Dim and very cool;

Till a wind or water wrinkle,
       Dipping marten, plumping trout,
Spreads in a twinkle
       And blots all out.

See the rings pursue each other;
       All below grows black as night,
Just as if mother
       Had blown out the light!

Patience, children, just a minute—
       See the spreading circles die;
The stream and all in it
       Will clear by-and-by.

Robert Louis Stevenson (1850–1894)

My River Runs to Thee

My River runs to thee.
Blue sea, wilt thou welcome me?
My river awaits reply.
Oh! Sea, look graciously.

I'll fetch thee brooks
From spotted nooks.
Say, sea,
Take me!

Emily Dickinson (1830–1886)

The Nile

It flows through old hushed Egypt and its sands,
  Like some grave mighty thought threading a
   dream,
  And times and things, as in that vision, seem
Keeping along it their eternal stands –
Caves pillars, pyramids, the shepherd bands
  That roamed through the young world, the
   glory extreme
  Of high Sesostris, and that southern beam,
The laughing queen that caught the world's great
 hands.
Then comes a mightier silence, stern and strong,
As of a world left empty of its throng,
  And the void weighs on us; and then we wake,
And hear the fruitful stream lapsing along
  'Twixt villages, and think how we shall take
  Our own calm journey on for human sake.

Leigh Hunt (1784–1859)

SONG OF THE BROOK:
STREAMS AND BROOKS

Song of the Brook

I come from haunts of coot and hern,
I make a sudden sally
And sparkle out among the fern,
To bicker down a valley.

By thirty hills I hurry down,
Or slip between the ridges,
By twenty thorpes, a little town,
And half a hundred bridges.

Till last by Philip's farm I flow
To join the brimming river,
For men may come and men may go,
But I go on for ever.

I chatter over stony ways,
In little sharps and trebles,
I bubble into eddying bays,
I babble on the pebbles.

With many a curve my banks I fret
By many a field and fallow,
And many a fairy foreland set
With willow-weed and mallow.

I chatter, chatter, as I flow
To join the brimming river,
For men may come and men may go,
But I go on for ever.

I wind about, and in and out,
With here a blossom sailing,
And here and there a lusty trout,
And here and there a grayling,

And here and there a foamy flake
Upon me, as I travel
With many a silvery waterbreak
Above the golden gravel,

And draw them all along, and flow
To join the brimming river
For men may come and men may go,
But I go on for ever.

I steal by lawns and grassy plots,
I slide by hazel covers;
I move the sweet forget-me-nots
That grow for happy lovers.

I slip, I slide, I gloom, I glance,
Among my skimming swallows;
I make the netted sunbeam dance
Against my sandy shallows.

I murmur under moon and stars
In brambly wildernesses;
I linger by my shingly bars;
I loiter round my cresses;

And out again I curve and flow
To join the brimming river,
For men may come and men may go,
But I go on for ever.

Alfred, Lord Tennyson (1809–1892)

Sonnet

There is a little unpretending Rill
Of limpid water, humbler far than aught
That ever among Men or Naiads sought
Notice or name! – It quivers down the hill,
Furrowing its shallow way with dubious will;
Yet to my mind this scanty stream is brought
Oftener than Ganges or the Nile; a thought
Of private recollection sweet and still!
Months perish with their moons; year treads on year;
But, faithful Emma! thou with me canst say
That, while ten thousand pleasures disappear,
And flies their memory fast as almost they;
The immortal Spirit of one happy day
Lingers beside that Rill, in vision clear.

William Wordsworth (1770–1850)

Water

The water understands
Civilization well;
It wets my foot, but prettily,
It chills my life, but wittily,
It is not disconcerted,
It is not broken-hearted:
Well used, it decketh joy,
Adorneth, doubleth joy:
Ill used, it will destroy,
In perfect time and measure
With a face of golden pleasure
Elegantly destroy.

Ralph Waldo Emerson (1803–1882)

Rivulet

By the sad purling of some rivulet
    O'er which the bending yew and willow grow,
That scarce the glimmerings of the day permit
    To view the melancholy banks below,
Where dwells no noise but what the murmurs make,
When the unwilling stream the shade forsakes.

Aphra Behn (1640–1689)

The Brook

Seated once by a brook, watching a child
Chiefly that paddled, I was thus beguiled.
Mellow the blackbird sang and sharp the thrush
Not far off in the oak and hazel brush,
Unseen. There was a scent like honeycomb
From mugwort dull. And down upon the dome
Of the stone the cart-horse kicks against so oft
A butterfly alighted. From aloft
He took the heat of the sun, and from below.
On the hot stone he perched contented so,
As if never a cart would pass again
That way; as if I were the last of men
And he the first of insects to have earth
And sun together and know their worth.
I was divided between him and the gleam,
The motion, and the voices, of the stream,
The waters running frizzled over gravel,
That never vanish and for ever travel.
A grey flycatcher silent on a fence
And I sat as if we had been there since
The horseman and the horse lying beneath
The fir-tree-covered barrow on the heath,
The horseman and the horse with silver shoes,
Galloped the downs last. All that I could lose
I lost. And then the child's voice raised the dead.
'No one's been here before' was what she said
And what I felt, yet never should have found
A word for, while I gathered sight and sound.

Edward Thomas (1878–1917)

Song

The feathers of the willow
Are half of them grown yellow
    Above the swelling stream;
And ragged are the bushes,
And rusty now the rushes,
    And wild the clouded gleam.

The thistle now is older,
His stalk begins to moulder,
    His head is white as snow;
The branches are all barer,
The linnet's song is rarer,
    The robin pipeth now.

Richard Watson Dixon (1833–1900)

from Ode

Intimations of Immortality from
Recollections of Early Childhood

There was a time when meadow, grove and stream,
The earth, and every common sight,
        To me did seem
      Apparelled in celestial light,
The glory and the freshness of a dream.
It is not now as it hath been of yore;
        Turn wheresoe'er I may,
        By night or day,
The things which I have seen I now can see no more.

          The Rainbow comes and goes,
          And lovely is the Rose;
          The Moon doth with delight
Look round her when the heavens are bare;
          Waters on a starry night
          Are beautiful and fair;
    The sunshine is a glorious birth;
    But yet I know, where'er I go,
That there hath passes away a glory from the earth.

William Wordsworth (1770–1850)

Sonnet to a River Otter

Dear native brook! wild streamlet of the West!
How many various-fated years have passed,
What happy and what mournful hours, since last
I skimmed the smooth thin stone along thy breast,
Numbering its light leaps! Yet so deep impressed
Sink the sweet scenes of childhood, that mine eyes
I never shut amid the sunny ray,
But straight with all their tints thy waters rise,
Thy crossing plank, thy marge with willows grey,
And bedded sand that, veined with various dyes,
Gleamed through thy bright transparence! On my way,
Visions of childhood! oft have ye beguiled
Lone manhood's cares, yet waking fondest sighs:
Ah! that once more I were a careless child!

Samuel Taylor Coleridge (1772–1834)

The Water Is Wide

The water is wide, I can't swim o'er
Nor do I have wings to fly
Give me a boat that can carry two
And both shall row, my love and I

A ship there is and she sails the sea
She's loaded deep as deep can be
But not so deep as the love I'm in
I know not if I sink or swim

I leaned my back against an oak
Thinking it was a trusty tree
But first it swayed and then it broke
So did my love prove false to me

Oh love is handsome and love is kind
Sweet as flower when first it is new
But love grows old and waxes cold
And fades away like the morning dew

Must I go bound while you go free
Must I love a man who doesn't love me
Must I be born with so little art
As to love a man who'll break my heart

Anon.

Cavalry Crossing a Ford

A line in long array, where they wind betwixt green
   islands;
They take a serpentine course – their arms flash in
   the sun –
      hark to the musical clank;
Behold the silvery river – in it the splashing horses,
   loitering, stop
      to drink;
Behold the brown-faced men – each group, each
   person, a
      picture – the negligent rest on the saddles;
Some emerge on the opposite bank – others are just
   entering the
      ford – while,
Scarlet, and blue, and snowy white,
The guidon flags flutter gaily in the wind.

Walt Whitman (1819–1892)

In Romney Marsh

As I went down to Dymchurch Wall,
  I heard the South sing o'er the land
I saw the yellow sunlight fall
  On knolls where Norman churches stand.

And ringing shrilly, taunt and lithe,
  Within the wind a core of sound,
The wire from Romney town to Hythe
  Along its airy journey wound.

A veil of purple vapour flowed
  And trailed its fringe along the Straits;
The upper air like sapphire glowed:
  And roses filled Heaven's central gates.

Masts in the offing wagged their tops;
  The swinging waves pealed on the shore;
The saffron beach, all diamond drops
  And beads of surge, prolonged the roar.

As I came up from Dymchurch Wall,
  I saw above the Downs' low crest
The crimson brands of sunset fall,
  Flicker and fade from out the West.

Night sank: like flakes of silver fire
  The stars in one great shower came down;
Shrill blew the wind; and shrill the wire
  Rang out from Hythe to Romney town.

The darkly shining salt sea drops
   Streamed as the waves clashed on the shore;
The beach, with all its organ stops
   Pealing again, prolonged the roar.

John Davidson (1857–1909)

Heaven

Fish (fly-replete, in depth of June,
Dawdling away their wat'ry noon)
Ponder deep wisdom, dark or clear,
Each secret fishy hope or fear.
Fish say, they have their Stream and Pond;
But is there anything Beyond?
This life cannot be All, they swear,
For how unpleasant, if it were!
One may not doubt that, somehow, Good
Shall come of Water and of Mud;
And, sure, the reverent eye must see
A Purpose in Liquidity.
We darkly know, by Faith we cry,
The future is not Wholly Dry.
Mud unto mud! – Death eddies near –
Not here the appointed End, not here!
But somewhere, beyond Space and Time,
Is wetter water, slimier slime!
And there (they trust) there swimmeth One
Who swam ere rivers were begun,
Immense, of fishy form and mind,
Squamous, omnipotent, and kind;
And under that Almighty Fin,
The littlest fish may enter in.
Oh! never fly conceals a hook,
Fish say, in the Eternal Brook,
But more than mundane weeds are there,
And mud, celestially fair;
Fat caterpillars drift around,
And Paradisal grubs are found;

Unfading moths, immortal flies,
And the worm that never dies.
And in that Heaven of all their wish,
There shall be no more land, say fish.

Rupert Brooke (1887–1915)

The Waterfall

With what deep murmurs through time's silent stealth
Doth thy transparent, cool and watery wealth
    Here flowing fall,
      And chide, and call,
As if his liquid, loose retinue stayed
Ling'ring, and were of this steep place afraid,
    The common pass
    Where, clear as glass,
    All must descend
    Not to an end:
But quickened by this deep and rocky grave,
Rise to a longer course more bright and brave.
Dear stream! dear bank, where often I
Have sat, and pleased my pensive eye,
Why, since each drop of thy quick store
Runs thither, whence it flowed before,
Should poor souls fear a shade or night,
Who came (sure) from a sea of light?

Henry Vaughan (c.1622–1695)

The Cataract of Lodore

"How does the water
Come down at Lodore?"
My little boy asked me
Thus, once on a time;
And moreover he tasked me
To tell him in rhyme.
Anon, at the word,
There first came one daughter,
And then came another,
To second and third
The request of their brother,
And to hear how the water
Comes down at Lodore,
With its rush and its roar,
As many a time
They had seen it before.
So I told them in rhyme,
For of rhymes I had store;
And 'twas in my vocation
For their recreation
That so I should sing;
Because I was Laureate
To them and the King.

From its sources which well
In the tarn on the fell;
From its fountains
In the mountains,
Its rills and its gills;
Through moss and through brake,
It runs and it creeps

For a while, till it sleeps
In its own little lake.
And thence at departing,
Awakening and starting,
It runs through the reeds,
And away it proceeds,
Through meadow and glade,
In sun and in shade,
And through the wood-shelter,
Among crags in its flurry,
Helter-skelter,
Hurry-skurry.
Here it comes sparkling,
And there it lies darkling;
Now smoking and frothing
Its tumult and wrath in,
Till, in this rapid race
On which it is bent,
It reaches the place
Of its steep descent.

The cataract strong
Then plunges along,
Striking and raging

As if a war raging
Its caverns and rocks among;
Rising and leaping,
Sinking and creeping,
Swelling and sweeping,
Showering and springing,
Flying and flinging,
Writhing and ringing,
Eddying and whisking,

Spouting and frisking,
Turning and twisting,
Around and around
With endless rebound:
Smiting and fighting,
A sight to delight in;
Confounding, astounding,
Dizzying and deafening the ear with its sound.

Collecting, projecting,
Receding and speeding,
And shocking and rocking,
And darting and parting,
And threading and spreading,
And whizzing and hissing,
And dripping and skipping,
And hitting and splitting,
And shining and twining,
And rattling and battling,
And shaking and quaking,
And pouring and roaring,
And waving and raving,
And tossing and crossing,
And flowing and going,
And running and stunning,
And foaming and roaming,
And dinning and spinning,
And dropping and hopping,
And working and jerking,
And guggling and struggling,
And heaving and cleaving,
And moaning and groaning;
And glittering and frittering,
And gathering and feathering,

And whitening and brightening,
And quivering and shivering,
And hurrying and skurrying,
And thundering and floundering;

Dividing and gliding and sliding,
And falling and brawling and sprawling,
And driving and riving and striving,
And sprinkling and twinkling and wrinkling,
And sounding and bounding and rounding,
And bubbling and troubling and doubling,
And grumbling and rumbling and tumbling,
And clattering and battering and shattering;

Retreating and beating and meeting and sheeting,
Delaying and straying and playing and spraying,
Advancing and prancing and glancing and dancing,
Recoiling, turmoiling and toiling and boiling,
And gleaming and streaming and steaming and
          beaming,
And rushing and flushing and brushing and gushing,
And flapping and rapping and clapping and slapping,
And curling and whirling and purling and twirling,
And thumping and plumping and bumping and
          jumping,
And dashing and flashing and splashing and clashing;
And so never ending, but always descending,
Sounds and motions for ever and ever are blending
All at once and all o'er, with a mighty uproar, –
And this way the water comes down at Lodore.

Robert Southey (1774–1843)

O TO SAIL:
SHIPS AND BOATS

O to sail

O to sail in a ship,
To leave this steady unendurable land,
To leave the tiresome sameness of the streets, the
      sidewalks and the houses,
To leave you, O you solid motionless land, and
      entering a ship,
To sail and sail and sail!

Walt Whitman (1819–1892)

Cargoes

Quinquireme of Nineveh from distant Ophir
Rowing home to haven in sunny Palestine,
With a cargo of ivory,
And apes and peacocks,
Sandalwood, cedarwood, and sweet white wine.

Stately Spanish galleon coming from the Isthmus,
Dipping through the Tropics by the palm-green shores,
With a cargo of diamonds,
Emeralds, amethysts,
Topazes, and cinnamon, and gold moidores.

Dirty British coaster with a salt-caked smoke stack
Butting through the Channel in the mad March days,
With a cargo of Tyne coal,
Road-rail, pig-lead,
Firewood, iron-ware, and cheap tin trays.

John Masefield (1878–1967)

Sail Away

Early in the day it was whispered that we should sail
   in a boat,
only thou and I, and never a soul in the world would
   know of this our
pilgrimage to no country and to no end.

In that shoreless ocean,
at thy silently listening smile my songs would swell in
   melodies,
free as waves, free from all bondage of words.

Is the time not come yet?
Are there works still to do?
Lo, the evening has come down upon the shore
and in the fading light the seabirds come flying to
   their nests.

Who knows when the chains will be off,
and the boat, like the last glimmer of sunset,
vanish into the night?

Rabindranath Tagore (1861–1941)

Where Go the Boats

Dark brown is the river.
Golden is the sand.
It flows along for ever,
With trees on either hand.
Green leaves a-floating,
Castles of the foam,
Boats of mine a-boating—
Where will all come home?
On goes the river
And out past the mill,
Away down the valley,
Away down the hill.
Away down the river,
A hundred miles or more,
Other little children
Shall bring my boats ashore.

Robert Louis Stevenson (1850–1894)

I Had a Boat

I had a boat, and the boat had wings;
    And I did dream that we went a flying
Over the heads of queens and kings,
    Over the souls of dead and dying,
Up among the stars and the great white rings,
    And where the Moon on her back is lying.

Mary Elizabeth Coleridge (1861–1907)

The Big Ship Sails on the Alley, Alley O

The big ship sails on the alley, alley O,
    The alley, alley O, the alley, alley O.
The big ship sails on the alley, alley O,
    On the last day of September,

The Captain said, 'This will never, never do,
    Never never do, never never do.'
The Captain said, 'This will never, never do,'
    On the last day of September.

The big ship sank to the bottom of the sea,
    The bottom of the sea, the bottom of the sea.
The big ship sank to the bottom of the sea,
    On the last day of September.

We all dip our heads in the deep blue sea,
    The deep blue sea, the deep blue sea.
We all dip our heads in the deep blue sea,
    On the last day of September.

Anon.

Song

The boat is chafing at our long delay,
    And we must leave too soon
The spicy sea-pinks and the inborne spray,
    The tawny sands, the moon.
Keep us, O Thetis, in our western flight!
    Watch from thy pearly throne
Our vessel, plunging deeper into night
    To reach a land unknown.

John Davidson (1857–1909)

Song

from The Tempest

The master, the swabber, the boatswain and I,
    The gunner and his mate,
Loved Mall, Meg, and Marian, and Margery,
    But none of us cared for Kate.
    For she had a tongue with a tang,
    Would cry to a sailor, 'Go hang!'
She loved not the savour of tar nor of pitch,
Yet a tailor might scratch her where'er she did itch.
    Then to sea, boys, and let her go hang.

William Shakespeare (1564–1616)

The Winds of Fate

One ship drives east and another drives west
With the selfsame winds that blow.
'Tis the set of the sails
And not of the gales
Which tells us the way to go.

Like the winds of the sea are the ways of fate,
As we voyage along through life;
'Tis the set of a soul
That decides its goal,
And not the calm or the strife

Ella Wheeler Wilcox (1850–1919)

Qua Cursum Ventus

As ships, becalmed at eve, that lay,
    With canvas drooping, side by side,
Two towers of sail at dawn of day
    Are scarce long leagues apart descried;
When fell the night, upsprung the breeze,
    And all the darkling hours they plied,
Nor dreamt but each the self-same seas
    By each was cleaving, side by side:
E'en so—but why the tale reveal
    Of those, whom year by year unchanged,
Brief absence joined anew to feel,
    Astounded, soul from soul estranged?
At dead of night their sails were filled,
    And onward each rejoicing steered:
Ah! neither blame, for neither willed
    Or wist, what first with dawn appeared.
To veer, how vain! On, onward strain,
    Brave barks! In light, in darkness too,
Through winds and tides one compass guides:
    To that, and your own selves, be true.
But O blithe breeze! and O great seas!
    Though ne'er, that earliest parting past,
On your wide plain they join again,
    Together lead them home at last!
One port, methought, alike they sought,
One purpose hold where'er they fare:
O bounding breeze, O rushing seas!
At last, at last, unite them there!

Arthur Hugh Clough (1819–1861)

In Praise of Fidelia

Get thee a ship well-rigged and tight,
With ordnance store, and manned for fight,
Snug in her timbers' mould for the seas,
Yet large in hold for merchandise;
Spread forth her cloth, and anchors weigh,
And let her on the curled waves play,
Till, fortune-towed, she chance to meet
Th' Hesperian home-bound Western Fleet;
Then let her board 'em, and for price
Take gold ore, sugar-canes, and spice:
     Yet when all these she hath brought ashore,
     In my fidelia I'll find more.

Mildmay Fane, Earl of Westmorland (1602–1666)

In Cabin'd Ships at Sea

In cabin'd ships at sea,
The boundless blue on every side expanding,
With whistling winds and music of the waves, the
      large imperious waves,
Or some lone bark buoy'd on the dense marine,
Where joyous full of faith, spreading white sails,
She cleaves the ether mid the sparkle and the foam of
      day, or under many a star at night,
By sailors young and old haply will I, a reminiscence
      of the land, be read,
In full rapport at last.

Here are our thoughts, voyagers' thoughts.
Here not the land, firm land, alone appears, may then by
      them be said.
The sky o'erarches here, we feel the undulating deck
      beneath our feet,
We feel the long pulsation, ebb and flow of endless motion,
The tones of unseen mystery, the vague and vast
      suggestions of the briny world, the liquid-flowing
      syllables,
The perfume, the faint creaking of the cordage, the
      melancholy rhythm,
The boundless vista and the horizon far and dim are all
      here.
And this is ocean's poem.

Then falter not O book, fulfil your destiny.
You not a reminiscence of the land alone,
You too as a lone bark cleaving the ether, purpos'd I
      know not whither, yet ever full of faith,

Consort to every ship that sails, sail you!
Bear forth to them folded my love, (dear mariners, for
	you I fold it here in every leaf;)
Speed on my book! spread your white sails my little
	bark athwart the imperious waves,
Chant on, sail on, bear o'er the boundless blue from
	me to every sea,
The song for mariners and all their ships.

Walt Whitman (1819–1892)

Boat Song

'Hail to the chief who in triumph advances!
      Honoured and blessed be the evergreen Pine!
Long may the tree, in his banner that glances,
      Flourish, the shelter and grace of our line!
          Heaven send it happy dew,
          Earth lend it sap anew,
Gayly to bourgeon, and broadly to grow,
          While every Highland glen
          Sends our shout back agen,
Roderigh Vich Alpine, dhu, ho! ieroe!

'Ours is no sapling, chance-sown by the fountain,
      Blooming at Beltane, in winter to fade;
When the whirlwind has stripped every leaf on the
      mountain,
      The more shall Clan-Alpine exult in her shade.
          Moored in the rifted rock,
          Proof to the tempest's shock,
Firmer he roots him the ruder it blow;
          Menteith and Breadalbane, then,
          Echo his praise agen,
Roderigh Vich Alpine dhu, ho! ieroe!

'Proudly our pibroch has thrilled in Glen Fruin,
      And Bannochar's groans to our slogan replied;
Glen Luss and Ross-dhu, they are smoking in ruin,
      And the best of Loch Lomond lie dead on
      her side.
          Widow and Saxon maid
          Long shall lament our raid,

Think of Clan-Alpine with fear and with woe;
  Lennox and Leven-glen
  Shake when they hear agen,
Roderigh Vich Alpine dhu, ho! ieroe!

'Row, vassals, row, for the pride of the Highlands!
  Stretch to your oars, for the evergreen Pine!
O! that the rose-bud that graces yon islands
  Were wreathed in a garland around him to twine!
   O that some seedling gem,
   Worthy such noble stem,
Honoured and blessed in their shadow might grow!
   Loud should Clan-Alpine then
   Ring from her deepmost glen,
Roderigh Vich Alpine dhu, ho! ieroe!'

Sir Walter Scott (1771–1832)

Canadian Boat Song

Listen to me, as when you heard our fathers
Sing long ago the song of other shores –
Listen to me, and then in chorus gather
All your deep voices, as ye pull your oars.

Chorus

> Fair these broad meads – these hoary woods
>   are grand;
> But we are exiles from our fathers' land.

From the lone sheiling of the misty island
Mountains divide us, and the waste of seas –
Yet still the blood is strong, the heart is Highland,
And we in dreams behold the Hebrides.

Chorus

> Fair these broad meads – these hoary woods
>   are grand;
> But we are exiles from our fathers' land.

We ne'er shall tread the fancy-haunted valley,
Where 'tween the dark hills creeps the small clear
    stream,
In arms around the patriarch banner rally,
Nor see the moon on royal tombstones gleam.

Chorus

> Fair these broad meads – these hoary woods
>   are grand;
> But we are exiles from our fathers' land.

When the bold kindred, in the time long vanish'd,
Conquered the soil and fortified the keep –
No seer foretold the children would be banish'd
That a degenerate lord might boast his sheep.

Chorus

> Fair these broad meads – these hoary woods
> are grand;
> But we are exiles from our fathers' land.

Come foreign rage – let Discord burst in slaughter!
O then for clansmen true, and stern claymore –
The hearts that would have given their blood like
water
Beat heavily beyond the Atlantic roar.

Anon.

The Inchcape Rock

No stir in the air, no stir in the sea,
The Ship was still as she could be;
Her sails from heaven received no motion,
Her keel was steady in the ocean.

Without either sign or sound of their shock,
The waves flow'd over the Inchcape Rock;
So little they rose, so little they fell,
They did not move the Inchcape Bell.

The Abbot of Aberbrothok
Had placed that bell on the Inchcape Rock;
On a buoy in the storm it floated and swung,
And over the waves its warning rung.

When the Rock was hid by the surge's swell,
The Mariners heard the warning Bell;
And then they knew the perilous Rock,
And blest the Abbot of Aberbrothok.

The Sun in the heaven was shining gay,
All things were joyful on that day;
The sea-birds scream'd as they wheel'd round,
And there was joyaunce in their sound.

The buoy of the Inchcape Bell was seen
A darker speck on the ocean green;
Sir Ralph the Rover walk'd his deck,
And fix'd his eye on the darker speck.

He felt the cheering power of spring,
It made him whistle, it made him sing;
His heart was mirthful to excess,
But the Rover's mirth was wickedness.

His eye was on the Inchcape Float;
Quoth he, 'My men, put out the boat,
And row me to the Inchcape Rock,
And I'll plague the Abbot of Aberbrothok.'

The boat is lower'd, the boatmen row,
And to the Inchcape Rock they go;
Sir Ralph bent over from the boat,
And he cut the Bell from the Inchcape Float.

Down sank the Bell with a gurgling sound,
The bubbles rose and burst around;
Quoth Sir Ralph, 'The next who comes to the Rock,
Won't bless the Abbot of Aberbrothok.'

Sir Ralph the Rover sail'd away,
He scour'd the seas for many a day;
And now grown rich with plunder'd store,
He steers his course for Scotland's shore.

So thick a haze o'erspreads the sky,
They cannot see the sun on high;
The wind hath blown a gale all day,
At evening it hath died away.

On the deck the Rover takes his stand,
So dark it is they see no land.
Quoth Sir Ralph, 'It will be lighter soon,
For there is the dawn of the rising Moon.'

'Canst hear,' said one, 'the breakers roar?
For methinks we should be near the shore.'
'Now, where we are I cannot tell,
But I wish we could hear the Inchcape Bell.'

They hear no sound, the swell is strong,
Though the wind hath fallen they drift along;
Till the vessel strikes with a shivering shock,
'Oh Christ! It is the Inchcape Rock!'

Sir Ralph the Rover tore his hair,
He curst himself in his despair;
The waves rush in on every side,
The ship is sinking beneath the tide.

But even in his dying fear,
One dreadful sound could the Rover hear;
A sound as if with the Inchcape Bell,
The Devil below was ringing his knell.

Robert Southey (1774–1843)

A St Kilda Lament

It was no crew of landsmen
Crossed the ferry on Wednesday:
'Tis tidings of disaster if you live not.

What has kept you so long from me?
Are the high sea and the sudden wind catching you,
So that you could not at once give her sail?

'Tis a profitless journey
That took the noble men away,
To take our one son from me and from Donald.

My son and my three brothers are gone,
And the one son of my mother's sister,
And, sorest tale, that will come or has come, my
  husband.

What has set me to draw ashes
And to take a spell at digging
Is that the men are away with no word of their living.

I am left without fun or merriment
Sitting on the floor of the glen;
My eyes are wet, oft are tears on them.

Anon.

The Skye Boat Song

Speed bonnie boat like a bird on the wing
Onward the sailors cry
Carry the lad that's born to be king
Over the sea to Skye

Loud the wind howls, loud the waves roar,
Thunderclaps rend the air
Baffled our foes, stand by the shore
Follow they will not dare

Speed bonnie boat like a bird on the wing
Onward the sailors cry
Carry the lad that's born to be king
Over the sea to Skye

Though the waves heave, soft will ye sleep
Ocean's a royal bed
Rocked in the deep, Flora will keep
Watch by your weary head

Speed bonnie boat like a bird on the wing
Onward the sailors cry
Carry the lad that's born to be king
Over the sea to Skye

Many's the lad that fought on that day
Well the claymore did wield
When the night came, silently lain
Dead on Culloden field

Speed bonnie boat like a bird on the wing
Onward the sailors cry
Carry the lad that's born to be king
Over the sea to Skye

Burned are our home, exile and death
Scatter the loyal men
Yet e'er the sword cool in the sheath
Charlie will come again.

Speed bonnie boat like a bird on the wing
Onward the sailors cry
Carry the lad that's born to be king
Over the sea to Skye.

Harold Boulton (1859–1935)

Sing me a Song of a Lad that is Gone

Mull was astern, Rum on the port,
Eigg on the starboard bow;
Glory of youth glowed in his soul:
Where is that glory now?

Chorus

  Sing me a song of a lad that is gone,
  Say, could that lad be I?
  Merry of soul he sailed on a day
  Over the sea to Skye.

Give me again all that was there,
Give me the sun that shone!
Give me the eyes, give me the soul,
Give me the lad that's gone!

Chorus

  Sing me a song of a lad that is gone,
  Say, could that lad be I?
  Merry of soul he sailed on a day
  Over the sea to Skye.

Billow and breeze, islands and sea,
Mountains of rain and sun,
All that was good, all that was fair,
All that was me is gone.

Sing me a song of a lad that is gone,
Say, could that lad be I?
Merry of soul he sailed on a day
Over the sea to Skye.

Robert Louis Stevenson (1850–1894)

Theme: Pride, arrogant, foolish will hurt you.
Man vs. Nature

The Wreck of the Hesperus
A Ballad

It was the schooner Hesperus,
    That sailed the wintry sea;
And the skipper had taken his little daughter,
    To bear him company.

Blue were her eyes as the fairy-flax,
    Her cheeks like the dawn of day,
And her bosom white as the hawthorn buds,
    That ope in the month of May.

The skipper he stood beside the helm,
    His pipe was in his mouth,
And he watched how the veering flaw did blow
    The smoke now West, now South.

Then up and spake an old Sailòr,
    Had sailed to the Spanish Main,
"I pray thee, put into yonder port,
    For I fear a hurricane.

"Last night, the moon had a golden ring,
    And to-night no moon we see!"
The skipper, he blew a whiff from his pipe,
    And a scornful laugh laughed he.

Colder and louder blew the wind,
    A gale from the Northeast,
The snow fell hissing in the brine,
    And the billows frothed like yeast.

156

Down came the storm, and smote amain
          The vessel in its strength;
She shuddered and paused, like a frighted steed,
          Then leaped her cable's length.

"Come hither! come hither! my little daughtèr,
          And do not tremble so;
For I can weather the roughest gale
          That ever wind did blow."

He wrapped her warm in his seaman's coat
          Against the stinging blast;
He cut a rope from a broken spar,
          And bound her to the mast.

"O father! I hear the church-bells ring,
          Oh say, what may it be?"
"'T is a fog-bell on a rock-bound coast!"—
          And he steered for the open sea.

"O father! I hear the sound of guns,
          Oh say, what may it be?"
"Some ship in distress, that cannot live
          In such an angry sea!"

"O father! I see a gleaming light,
          Oh say, what may it be?"
But the father answered never a word,
          A frozen corpse was he.

Lashed to the helm, all stiff and stark,
          With his face turned to the skies,
The lantern gleamed through the gleaming snow
          On his fixed and glassy eyes.

157

Then the maiden clasped her hands and prayed
That savèd she might be;
And she thought of Christ, who stilled the wave
On the Lake of Galilee.

And fast through the midnight dark and drear,
Through the whistling sleet and snow,
Like a sheeted ghost, the vessel swept
Tow'rds the reef of Norman's Woe.

And ever the fitful gusts between
A sound came from the land;
It was the sound of the trampling surf
On the rocks and the hard sea-sand.

The breakers were right beneath her bows,
She drifted a dreary wreck,
And a whooping billow swept the crew
Like icicles from her deck.

She struck where the white and fleecy waves
Looked soft as carded wool,
But the cruel rocks, they gored her side
Like the horns of an angry bull.

Her rattling shrouds, all sheathed in ice,
With the masts went by the board;
Like a vessel of glass, she stove and sank,
Ho! ho! the breakers roared!

At daybreak, on the bleak sea-beach,
A fisherman stood aghast,
To see the form of a maiden fair,
Lashed close to a drifting mast.

158

The salt sea was frozen on her breast,
    The salt tears in her eyes;
And he saw her hair, like the brown sea-weed,
    On the billows fall and rise.

Such was the wreck of the Hesperus,
    In the midnight and the snow!
Christ save us all from a death like this,
    On the reef of Norman's Woe!

Henry Wadsworth Longfellow (1807–1882)

The Flying Dutchman

Unyielding in the pride of his defiance,
    Afloat with none to serve or to command,
Lord of himself at last, and all by Science,
    He seeks the Vanished Land.

Alone, by the one light of his one thought,
    He steers to find the shore from which we came,
Fearless of in what coil he may be caught
    On seas that have no name.

Into the night he sails; and after night
    There is a dawning, though there be no sun;
Wherefore, with nothing but himself in sight,
    Unsighted, he sails on.

At last there is a lifting of the cloud
    Between the flood before him and the sky;
And then—though he may curse the Power aloud
    That has no power to die—

He steers himself away from what is haunted
    By the old ghost of what has been before,—
Abandoning, as always, and undaunted,
    One fog-walled island more.

Edwin Arlington Robinson (1869–1935)

Old Ironsides

Ay, tear her tattered ensign down!
Long has it waved on high,
And many an eye has danced to see
That banner in the sky;
Beneath it rung the battle shout,
And burst the cannon's roar; –
The meteor of the ocean air
Shall sweep the clouds no more!

Her deck, once red with heroes' blood,
Where knelt the vanquished foe,
When winds were hurrying o'er the flood,
And waves were white below,
No more shall feel the victor's tread,
Or know the conquered knee; –
The harpies of the shore shall pluck
The eagle of the sea!

O, better than her shattered hulk
Should sink beneath the wave;
Her thunders shook the mighty deep,
And there should be her grave;
Nail to the mast her holy flag,
Set every threadbare sail,
And give her to the god of storms,
The lightning and the gale!

Oliver Wendell Holmes (1809–1894)

Greenland Whale Fisheries

In eighteen hundred and forty-five,
Being March on the twentieth day,
Oh, we hoisted our colours to our topmost high
And for Greenland forged away, brave boys
And for Greenland forged away.

When we struck that Greenland shore
With our gallant ship in full fold,
We wished ourselves back safe home again
With our friends all on the same shore, brave boys
With our friends all on the shore.
Our mate stood on the forecastle yard
With a spyglass in his hand,
"There's a whake, there's a whale, there's a whale!"
    cried he,
"And she blows at every span, brave boys,
And she blows at every span."

Oh, when this whale we did harpoon
She made one slap with her tail,
She capsized our boat, we lost five of our crew,
Neither did we catch that whale, brave boys
Neither did we catch that whale.
"Sad news, sad news," to our captain we cried,
Which grieved his heart in full store,
But the losing of five of his jolly, jolly crew,
Oh, it grieved him ten times more, brave boys,
Oh, that grieved him ten times more.

"Hist your anchors then, brave boys," said he,
"Let us leave this cold countery
Where the storm and the snow and the whalefish does
    blow,
And daylight's seldom seen, brave boys,
And daylight's seldom seen."

Anon.

Ships That Passed in the Night

Out in the sky the great dark clouds are massing;
　　I look far out into the pregnant night,
Where I can hear a solemn booming gun
　　And catch the gleaming of a random light,
That tells me that the ship I seek is passing, passing.

My tearful eyes my soul's deep hurt are glassing;
　　For I would hail and check that ship of ships.
I stretch my hands imploring, cry aloud,
　　My voice falls dead a foot from mine own lips,
And but its ghost doth reach that vessel, passing,
　　　　passing.

O Earth, O Sky, O Ocean, both surpassing,
　　O heart of mine, O soul that dreads the dark!
Is there no hope for me? Is there no way
　　That I may sight and check that speeding bark
Which out of sight and sound is passing, passing?

Paul Laurence Dunbar (1872–1906)

Homeward Bound

They will take us from the moorings, they will take us
   from the Bay,
     They will pluck us up to windward when we sail.
We shall hear the keen wind whistle, we shall feel the
   sting of spray,
     When we've dropped the deep-sea pilot o'er
      the rail.
Then it's Johnnie heave an' start her, then it's Johnnie
   roll and go;
     When the mates have picked the watches, there is
      little rest for Jack.
But we'll raise the good old chanty that the
   Homeward bounders know,
     For the girls have got the tow-rope, an' they're
      hauling in the slack

In the dusty streets and dismal, through the noises of
   the town,
     We can hear the West wind humming through the
      shrouds;
We can see the lightning leaping when the tropic suns
   go down,
     And the dapple of the shadows of the clouds.
And salt blood dances in us, to the tune of
   Homeward Bound,
     To the call to weary watches, to the sheet and to
      the tack.
When they bid us man the capstan how the hands will
   walk her round! –
     For the girls have got the tow-rope, an' they're
      hauling in the slack.

Through the sunshine of the tropics, round the bleak
and dreary Horn,
   Half across the little planet lies our way.
We shall leave the land behind us like a welcome
that's outworn
   When we see the reeling mastheads swing and
   sway.
Through the weather fair or stormy, in the calm and
in the gale,
   We shall heave and haul to help her, we shall hold
   her on her track,
And you'll hear the chorus rolling when the hands are
making sail,
   For the girls have got the tow-rope, an' they're
   hauling in the slack!

D. H. Rogers

The Mystic Blue

Out of the darkness, fretted sometimes in its sleeping,

Jets of sparks in fountains of blue come leaping

To sight, revealing a secret, numberless secrets
    keeping.

Sometimes the darkness trapped within a wheel

Runs into speed like a dream, the blue of the steel

Showing the rocking darkness now a-reel.

And out of the invisible, streams of bright blue drops

Rain from the showery heavens, and bright blue crops

Surge from the under-dark to their ladder-tops.

And all the manifold blue and joyous eyes,

The rainbow arching over in the skies,

New sparks of wonder opening in surprise.

All these pure things come foam and spray of the sea

Of Darkness abundant, which shaken mysteriously,

Breaks into dazzle of living, as dolphins that leap from
the sea

Of midnight shake it to fire, so the secret of death we
see.

D. H. *Lawrence* (1885–1930)

Emigravit

With sails full set, the ship her anchor weighs.
Strange names shine out beneath her figure head.
What glad farewells with eager eyes are said!
What cheer for him who goes, and him who stays!
Fair skies, rich lands, new homes, and untried days
Some go to seek: the rest but wait instead,
Watching the way wherein their comrades led,
Until the next stanch ship her flag doth raise.
Who knows what myriad colonies there are
Of fairest fields, and rich, undreamed-of gains
Thick planted in the distant shining plains
Which we call sky because they lie so far?
Oh, write of me, not 'Died in bitter pains,'
But 'Emigrated to another star!'

Helen Hunt Jackson (1830–1885)

Above the Dock

Above the quiet dock in mid night,
Tangled in the tall mast's corded height,
Hangs the moon. What seemed so far away
Is but a child's balloon, forgotten after play.

T. E. Hulme (1883–1917)

from Carmina Gadelica

Helmsman:	Blest be the boat.
Crew:	God the Father bless her.
Helmsman:	Blest be the boat.
Crew:	God the Son bless her.
Helmsman:	Blest be the boat.
Crew:	God the Spirit bless her.
All:	God the Father, God the Son, God the Spirit, Bless the boat.

Helmsman:	What can befall you And God the Father with you?
Crew:	No harm can befall us.
Helmsman:	What can befall you And God the Son with you?
Crew:	No harm can befall us.
Helmsman:	What can befall you And God the Spirit with you?
Crew:	No harm can befall us.
All:	God the Father, God the Son, God the Spirit, With us eternally.

Helmsman:	What can cause you anxiety And God of the elements over you?
Crew:	No anxiety can be ours.
Helmsman:	What can cause you anxiety And God of the elements over you?
Crew:	No anxiety can be ours.

Helmsman:	What can cause you anxiety
	And King of the elements over you?
Crew:	No anxiety can be ours.
Helmsman:	What can cause you anxiety
	And Spirit of the elements over you?
Crew:	No anxiety can be ours.
All:	The God of the elements,
	The King of the elements,
	The Spirit of the elements,
	Close over us,
	Ever eternally.

Anon. tr. Alexander Carmichael (1832–1912)

WILD NIGHTS!:
SEA WEATHER

Wild nights—Wild nights!

Wild nights—Wild nights!
Were I with thee
Wild nights should be
Our luxury!

Futile—the winds—
To a Heart in port—
Done with the Compass—
Done with the Chart!

Rowing in Eden—
Ah—the Sea!
Might I but moor—tonight—
In thee!

Emily Dickinson (1830–1886)

A Wet Winter

from A Midsummer Night's Dream

Therefore the winds, piping to us in vain,
As in revenge have sucked up from the sea
Contagious fogs: which, falling in the land,
Hath every pelting river made so proud
That they have overborne their continents.
The ox hath therefore stretched his yoke in vain,
The ploughman lost his sweat, and the green corn
Hath rotted ere his youth attained a beard.
The fold stands empty in the drownèd field,
And crows are fatted with the murrion flock,
The nine men's morris is filled up with mud,
And the quaint mazes in the wanton green
For lack of tread are undistinguishable.

William Shakespeare (1564–1616)

Deep-Sea Calm

With what deep calm, and passionlessly great,
Thy central soul is stored, the Equinox
Roars, and the North Wind drives ashore his flocks,
Thou heedest not, thou dost not feel the weight
Of the Leviathan, the ships in state
Plough on, and hull with hull in battle shocks,
Unshaken thou; the trembling planet rocks,
Yet thy deep heart will scarcely palpitate.
Peace-girdle of the world, thy face is moved,
And now thy furrowed brow with fierce light gleams,
Now laughter ripples forth a thousand miles,
But still the calm of thine abysmal streams
Flows round the people of our fretful isles,
And Earth's inconstant fever is reproved.

H. D. Rawnsley (1851–1920)

Les Silhouettes

The sea is flecked with bars of grey,
The dull dead wind is out of tune,
And like a withered leaf the moon
Is blown across the stormy bay.

Etched clear upon the pallid sand
The black boat lies: a sailor boy
Clambers aboard in careless joy
With laughing face and gleaming hand.

And overhead the curlews cry,
Where through the dusky upland grass
The young brown-throated reapers pass,
Like silhouettes against the sky.

Oscar Wilde (1854–1900)

On the Sea

It keeps eternal whisperings around
    Desolate shores, and with its mighty swell
    Gluts twice ten thousand caverns, till the spell
Of Hecate leaves them their old shadowy sound.
Often 'tis in such gentle temper found,
    That scarcely will the very smallest shell
    Be moved for days from whence it sometime
        fell,
When last the winds of heaven were unbound.
Oh ye! who have your eye-balls vexed and tired,
    Feast them upon the wideness of the Sea;
        Oh ye! whose ears are dinned with
          uproar rude,
    Or fed too much with cloying melody, –
        Sit ye near some old cavern's mouth,
          and brood
Until ye start, as if the sea-nymphs quired!

John Keats (1795–1821)

The Sound of the Sea

The sea awoke at midnight from its sleep,
    And round the pebbly beaches far and wide
    I heard the first wave of the rising tide
    Rush onward with uninterrupted sweep;
A voice out of the silence of the deep,
    A sound mysteriously multiplied
    As of a cataract from the mountain's side,
    Or roar of winds upon a wooded steep.
So comes to us at times, from the unknown
    And inaccessible solitudes of being,
    The rushing of the sea-tides of the soul;
And inspirations, that we deem our own,
    Are some divine foreshadowing and foreseeing
    Of things beyond our reason or control.

Henry Wadsworth Longfellow (1807–1882)

from The Storm

The south and west winds joined, and, as they blew,
Waves like a rolling trench before them threw.
Sooner than you read this line, did the gale,
Like shot, not feared till felt, our sails assail;
And what at first was called a gust, the same
Hath now a storm's, anon a tempest's name.
Jonas, I pity thee, and curse those men,
Who when the storm raged most, did wake thee then;
Sleep is pain's easiest salve, and doth fulfill
All offices of death, except to kill.
But when I waked, I saw, that I saw not;
Ay, and the sun, which should teach me, had forgot
East, west, day, night, and I could only say,
If the world had lasted, now it had been day.
Thousands our noises were, yet we 'mongst all
Could none by his right name, but thunder call.
Lightning was all our light, and it rained more
Than if the sun had drunk the sea before.
Some coffin'd in their cabins lie, equally
Grieved that they are not dead, and yet must die;
And as sin-burdened souls from graves will creep
At the last day, some forth their cabins peep:
And tremblingly ask "What news?" and do hear so,
Like jealous husbands, what they would not know.
Some sitting on the hatches, would seem there
With hideous gazing to fear away fear.
Then note they the ship's sicknesses, the mast
Shaked with this ague, and the hold and waist
With a salt dropsy clogged, and all our tacklings
Snapping, like too high stretched treble strings,
And from our tattered sails rags drop down so,

As from one hanged in chains, a year ago.
Even our ordnance placed for our defence,
Strive to break loose, and 'scape away from thence.
Pumping hath tired our men, and what's the gain?
Seas into seas thrown, we suck in again;
Hearing hath deaf'd our sailors, and if they
Knew how to hear, there's none knows what to say.
Compared to these storms death is but a qualm,
Hell somewhat lightsome, and the Bermudas calm.
Darkness, light's elder brother, his birthright
Claims o'er this world, and to heaven hath chased light.
All things are one, and that one none can be,
Since all forms uniform deformity
Doth cover; so that we, except God say
Another Fiat, shall have no more day:
So violent, yet long these furies be.

John Donne (1572–1631)

The Way of the Wind

The wind's way in the deep sky's hollow
None may measure, as none can say
How the heart in her shows the swallow
  The wind's way.

Hope nor fear can avail to stay
Waves that whiten on wrecks that wallow,
Times and seasons that wane and slay.

Life and love, till the strong night swallow
Thought and hope and the red last ray,
Swim the waters of years that follow
  The wind's way.

Algernon Charles Swinburne (1837–1909)

The Sea Limits

Consider the sea's listless chime:
    Time's self it is, made audible,—
    The murmur of the earth's own shell.
Secret continuance sublime
    Is the sea's end: our sight may pass
    No furlong further. Since time was,
This sound hath told the lapse of time.

No quiet, which is death's,—it hath
    The mournfulness of ancient life,
    Enduring always at dull strife.
As the world's heart of rest and wrath,
    Its painful pulse is in the sands.
    Last utterly, the whole sky stands,
Gray and not known, along its path.

Listen alone beside the sea,
    Listen alone among the woods;
    Those voices of twin solitudes
Shall have one sound alike to thee:
    Hark where the murmurs of thronged men
    Surge and sink back and surge again,—
Still the one voice of wave and tree.

Gather a shell from the strewn beach
    And listen at its lips: they sigh
    The same desire and mystery,

The echo of the whole sea's speech.
  And all mankind is thus at heart
  Not anything but what thou art:
And Earth, Sea, Man, are all in each.

   Dante Gabriel Rossetti (1828–1882)

At Melville's Tomb

Often beneath the wave, wide from this ledge,
The dice of drowned men's bones he saw bequeath
An embassy. Their numbers, as he watched,
Beat on the dusty shore and were obscured.

And wrecks passed without sound of bells,
The calyx of death's bounty giving back
A scattered chapter, livid hieroglyph,
The portent wound in corridors of shells.

Then in the circuit calm of one vast coil,
Its lashings charmed and malice reconciled,
Frosted eyes there were that lifted altars:
And silent answers crept across the stars.

Compass, quadrant and sextant contrive
No farther tides . . . High in the azure steeps
Monody shall not wake the mariner.
This fabulous shadow only the sea keeps.

Hart Crane (1899–1932)

The New Colossus

Not like the brazen giant of Greek fame,
With conquering limbs astride from land to land;
Here at our sea-washed, sunset gates shall stand
A mighty woman with a torch, whose flame
Is the imprisoned lightning, and her name
Mother of Exiles. From her beacon-hand
Glows world-wide welcome; her mild eyes command
The air-bridged harbor that twin cities frame.
'Keep, ancient lands, your storied pomp!' cries she
With silent lips. 'Give me your tired, your poor,
Your huddled masses yearning to breathe free,
The wretched refuse of your teeming shore.
Send these, the homeless, tempest-tost to me,
I lift my lamp beside the golden door!'

Emma Lazarus (1849–1887)

THE LAKE ISLE AT INNISFREE:
LAKES AND LOCHS

The Lake Isle of Innisfree

I will arise and go now, and go to Innisfree,
And a small cabin build there, of clay and wattles
   made:
Nine bean-rows will I have there, a hive for the
   honey-bee,
And live alone in the bee-loud glade.

And I shall have some peace there, for peace comes
   dropping slow,
Dropping from the veils of the morning to where the
   cricket sings;
There midnight's all a glimmer, and noon a purple
   glow,
And evening full of linnet's wings.

And I will arise and go now, for always night and day
I hear the lake water lapping with low sounds by the
   shore;
While I stand on the roadway, or on the pavements
   gray,
I hear it in the deep heart's core.

W. B. Yeats (1865–1939)

By lone St. Mary's silent lake

By lone St. Mary's silent lake:
Thou know'st it well,—nor fen nor sedge
Pollute the pure lake's crystal edge;
Abrupt and sheer, the mountains sink
At once upon the level brink;
And just a trace of silver sand
Marks where the water meets the land.
Far in the mirror, bright and blue,
Each hill's huge outline you may view;
Shaggy with heath, but lonely bare,
Nor tree, nor bush, nor brake, is there,
Save where, of land, yon slender line
Bears thwart the lake the scatter'd pine.
Yet even this nakedness has power,
And aids the feeling of the hour:
Nor thicket, dell, nor copse you spy,
Where living thing concealed might lie;
Nor point, retiring, hides a dell,
Where swain, or woodman lone, might dwell;
There's nothing left to fancy's guess,
You see that all is loneliness:
And silence aids—though the steep hills
Send to the lake a thousand rills;
In summer tide, so soft they weep,
The sound but lulls the ear asleep;
Your horse's hoof-tread sounds too rude,
So stilly is the solitude.

Sir Walter Scott (1771–1832)

from The Prelude

She was an elfin Pinnace; lustily
I dipp'd my oars into the silent Lake,
And, as I rose upon the stroke, my Boat
Went heaving through the water, like a Swan;
When from behind that craggy Steep, till then
The bound of the horizon, a huge Cliff,
As if with voluntary power instinct,
Uprear'd its head. I struck, and struck again
And, growing still in stature, the huge Cliff
Rose up between me and the stars, and still,
With measur'd motion, like a living thing,
Strode after me. With trembling hands I turn'd,
And through the silent water stole my way
Back to the Cavern of the Willow tree.
There, in her mooring-place, I left my Bark,
And, through the meadows homeward went, with grave
And serious thoughts; and after I had seen
That spectacle, for many days, my brain
Work'd with a dim and undetermin'd sense
Of unknown modes of being; in my thoughts
There was a darkness, call it solitude,
Or blank desertion, no familiar shapes
Of hourly objects, images of trees,
Of sea or sky, no colours of green fields;
But huge and mighty Forms that do not live
Like living men mov'd slowly through my mind
By day and were the trouble of my dreams.

William Wordsworth (1770–1850)

Loch Lomond

By yon bonnie banks and by yon bonnie braes
Where the sun shines bright on Loch Lomond
Where me and my true love were ever wont tae gae
On the bonnie, bonnie banks o' Loch Lomond.

Oh you tak' the high road and I'll tak the low road
An' I'll be in Scotland afore ye,
But me and my true love will never meet again
On the bonnie, bonnie banks o' Loch Lomond.

'Twas there that we parted in yon shady glen
On the steep, steep side of Ben Lomond,
Where in purple hue, the hieland hills we view,
And the moon comin' out in the gloamin'.

Oh you tak' the high road and I'll tak the low road
And I'll be in Scotland afore ye,
But me and my true love will never meet again
On the bonnie, bonnie banks o' Loch Lomond.

Oh you tak' the high road and I'll tak the low road
An' I'll be in Scotland afore ye,
But me and my true love will never meet again
On the bonnie, bonnie banks o' Loch Lomond.

Alicia Ann, Lady John Scott (1810–1900)

THE JUMBLIES:
SEASIDE FOLK

The Walrus and the Carpenter

"The sun was shining on the sea,
 Shining with all his might:
He did his very best to make
 The billows smooth and bright—
And this was odd, because it was
 The middle of the night.

The moon was shining sulkily,
 Because she thought the sun
Had got no business to be there
 After the day was done—
'It's very rude of him,' she said,
 'To come and spoil the fun.'

The sea was wet as wet could be,
 The sands were dry as dry.
You could not see a cloud, because
 No cloud was in the sky:
No birds were flying overhead—
 There were no birds to fly.

The Walrus and the Carpenter
 Were walking close at hand;
They wept like anything to see
 Such quantities of sand:
'If this were only cleared away,'
 They said, 'it *would* be grand!'

'If seven maids with seven mops
 Swept it for half a year,
Do you suppose,' the Walrus said,

'That they could get it clear?'
    'I doubt it,' said the Carpenter,
And shed a bitter tear.

'O Oysters, come and walk with us!'
    The Walrus did beseech.
'A pleasant walk, a pleasant talk,
    Along the briny beach:
We cannot do with more than four,
    To give a hand to each.'

The eldest Oyster looked at him,
    But never a word he said:
The eldest Oyster winked his eye,
    And shook his heavy head—
Meaning to say he did not choose
    To leave the oyster-bed.

But four young Oysters hurried up,
    All eager for the treat:
Their coats were brushed, their faces washed,
    Their shoes were clean and neat—
And this was odd, because, you know,
    They hadn't any feet.

Four other Oysters followed them,
    And yet another four;
And thick and fast they came at last,
    And more, and more, and more—
All hopping through the frothy waves,
    And scrambling to the shore.

The Walrus and the Carpenter
    Walked on a mile or so,

And then they rested on a rock
    Conveniently low:
And all the little Oysters stood
    And waited in a row.

'The time has come,' the Walrus said,
    'To talk of many things:
Of shoes—and ships—and sealing-wax—
    Of cabbages—and kings—
And why the sea is boiling hot—
    And whether pigs have wings.'

'But wait a bit,' the Oysters cried,
    'Before we have our chat;
For some of us are out of breath,
    And all of us are fat!'
'No hurry!' said the Carpenter.
    They thanked him much for that.

'A loaf of bread,' the Walrus said,
    'Is what we chiefly need:
Pepper and vinegar besides
    Are very good indeed—
Now if you're ready, Oysters dear,
    We can begin to feed.'

'But not on us!' the Oysters cried,
    Turning a little blue.
'After such kindness, that would be
    A dismal thing to do!'
'The night is fine,' the Walrus said.
    'Do you admire the view?

It was so kind of you to come!
    And you are very nice!'
The Carpenter said nothing but
    'Cut us another slice:
I wish you were not quite so deaf—
    I've had to ask you twice!'

'It seems a shame,' the Walrus said,
    'To play them such a trick,
After we've brought them out so far,
    And made them trot so quick!'
The Carpenter said nothing but
    'The butter's spread too thick!'

'I weep for you,' the Walrus said:
    'I deeply sympathize.'
With sobs and tears he sorted out
    Those of the largest size,
Holding his pocket-handkerchief
    Before his streaming eyes.

'O Oysters,' said the Carpenter,
    You've had a pleasant run!
Shall we be trotting home again?'
    But answer came there none—
And this was scarcely odd, because
    They'd eaten every one."

Lewis Carroll (1832–1898)

The Jumblies

I

They went to sea in a Sieve, they did,
In a Sieve they went to sea:
In spite of all their friends could say,
On a winter's morn, on a stormy day,
In a Sieve they went to sea!
And when the Sieve turned round and round,
And every one cried, 'You'll all be drowned!'
They called aloud, 'Our Sieve ain't big,
But we don't care a button! we don't care a fig!
In a Sieve we'll go to sea!'
Far and few, far and few,
Are the lands where the Jumblies live;
Their heads are green, and their hands are blue,
And they went to sea in a Sieve.

II

They sailed away in a Sieve, they did,
In a Sieve they sailed so fast,
With only a beautiful pea-green veil
Tied with a riband by way of a sail,
To a small tobacco-pipe mast;
And every one said, who saw them go,
'O won't they be soon upset, you know!
For the sky is dark, and the voyage is long,
And happen what may, it's extremely wrong
In a Sieve to sail so fast!'
Far and few, far and few,

Are the lands where the Jumblies live;
Their heads are green, and their hands are blue,
And they went to sea in a Sieve.

III

The water it soon came in, it did,
The water it soon came in;
So to keep them dry, they wrapped their feet
In a pinky paper all folded neat,
And they fastened it down with a pin.
And they passed the night in a crockery-jar,
And each of them said, 'How wise we are!
Though the sky be dark, and the voyage be long,
Yet we never can think we were rash or wrong,
While round in our Sieve we spin!'
Far and few, far and few,
Are the lands where the Jumblies live;
Their heads are green, and their hands are blue,
And they went to sea in a Sieve.

IV

And all night long they sailed away;
And when the sun went down,
They whistled and warbled a moony song
To the echoing sound of a coppery gong,
In the shade of the mountains brown.
'O Timballo! How happy we are,
When we live in a sieve and a crockery-jar,
And all night long in the moonlight pale,
We sail away with a pea-green sail,

In the shade of the mountains brown!'
Far and few, far and few,
Are the lands where the Jumblies live;
Their heads are green, and their hands are blue,
And they went to sea in a Sieve.

V

They sailed to the Western Sea, they did,
To a land all covered with trees,
And they bought an Owl, and a useful Cart,
And a pound of Rice, and a Cranberry Tart,
And a hive of silvery Bees.
And they bought a Pig, and some green Jack-daws,
And a lovely Monkey with lollipop paws,
And forty bottles of Ring-Bo-Ree,
And no end of Stilton Cheese.
Far and few, far and few,
Are the lands where the Jumblies live;
Their heads are green, and their hands are blue,
And they went to sea in a Sieve.

VI

And in twenty years they all came back,
In twenty years or more,
And every one said, 'How tall they've grown!'
For they've been to the Lakes, and the Torrible Zone,
And the hills of the Chankly Bore;
And they drank their health, and gave them a feast
Of dumplings made of beautiful yeast;
And everyone said, 'If we only live,

We too will go to sea in a Sieve,—
To the hills of the Chankly Bore!'
Far and few, far and few,
Are the lands where the Jumblies live;
Their heads are green, and their hands are blue,
And they went to sea in a Sieve.

Edward Lear (1812–1888)

The Owl and the Pussy-Cat

The Owl and the Pussy-Cat went to sea
    In a beautiful pea-green boat,
They took some honey, and plenty of money,
    Wrapped up in a five-pound note.
The Owl looked up to the stars above,
    And sang to a small guitar,
'O lovely Pussy! O Pussy, my love,
    What a beautiful Pussy you are,
        You are,
        You are!
    What a beautiful Pussy you are!'

Pussy said to the Owl, 'You elegant fowl!
    How charmingly sweet you sing!
O let us be married! too long we have tarried:
    But what shall we do for a ring?'
They sailed away, for a year and a day,
    To the land where the Bong-tree grows
And there in a wood a Piggy-wig stood
    With a ring at the end of his nose,
        His nose,
        His nose,
    With a ring at the end of his nose.

'Dear Pig, are you willing to sell for one shilling
    Your ring?' Said the Piggy, 'I will.'
So they took it away, and were married next day
    By the Turkey who lives on the hill.
They dined on mince, and slices of quince,
    Which they ate with a runcible spoon;

And hand in hand, on the edge of the sand,
  They danced by the light of the moon,
      The moon,
      The moon,
  They danced by the light of the moon.

Edward Lear (1812–1888)

The Sands of Dee

"O Mary, go and call the cattle home,
    And call the cattle home,
    And call the cattle home,
    Across the sands of Dee."
The western wind was wild and dark with foam,
    And all alone went she.

The western tide crept up along the sand,
    And o'er and o'er the sand
    And round and round the sand,
    As far as the eye could see.
The rolling mist came down and hid the land:
    And never home came she.
"O is it weed, or fish, or floating hair –
    A tress of golden hair
    A drownèd maiden's hair,
    Above the nets at sea?
Was never salmon yet shone so fair
    Among the stakes of Dee."

They row'd her in across the rolling foam,
    The cruel crawling foam,
    The cruel hungry foam,
    To her grave beside the sea.
But still the boatmen hear her call the cattle home,
    Across the sands of Dee.

Charles Kingsley (1819–1875)

The Lady of Shalott

PART I

On either side the river lie
Long fields of barley and of rye,
That clothe the wold and meet the sky;
And thro' the field the road runs by
To many-tower'd Camelot;
And up and down the people go,
Gazing where the lilies blow
Round an island there below,
The island of Shalott.

Willows whiten, aspens quiver,
Little breezes dusk and shiver
Thro' the wave that runs for ever
By the island in the river
Flowing down to Camelot.
Four grey walls, and four grey towers,
Overlook a space of flowers,
And the silent isle imbowers
The Lady of Shalott.

By the margin, willow veil'd
Slide the heavy barges trail'd
By slow horses; and unhail'd
The shallop flitteth silken-sail'd
Skimming down to Camelot:
But who hath seen her wave her hand?
Or at the casement seen her stand?
Or is she known in all the land,
The Lady of Shalott?

Only reapers, reaping early
In among the bearded barley,
Hear a song that echoes cheerly
From the river winding clearly,
Down to tower'd Camelot:
And by the moon the reaper weary,
Piling sheaves in uplands airy,
Listening, whispers " 'Tis the fairy
Lady of Shalott."

PART II

There she weaves by night and day
A magic web with colours gay.
She has heard a whisper say,
A curse is on her if she stay
To look down to Camelot.
She knows not what the curse may be,
And so she weaveth steadily,
And little other care hath she,
The Lady of Shalott.

And moving thro' a mirror clear
That hangs before her all the year,
Shadows of the world appear.
There she sees the highway near
Winding down to Camelot:
There the river eddy whirls,
And there the surly village-churls,
And the red cloaks of market girls,
Pass onward from Shalott.

Sometimes a troop of damsels glad,
An abbot on an ambling pad,
Sometimes a curly shepherd-lad,
Or long-hair'd page in crimson clad,
  Goes by to tower'd Camelot;
And sometimes thro' the mirror blue
The knights come riding two and two:
She hath no loyal knight and true,
  The Lady of Shalott.

But in her web she still delights
To weave the mirror's magic sights,
For often thro' the silent nights
A funeral, with plumes and lights,
  And music, went to Camelot:
Or when the moon was overhead,
Came two young lovers lately wed;
"I am half sick of shadows," said
  The Lady of Shalott.

PART III

A bow-shot from her bower-eaves,
He rode between the barley-sheaves,
The sun came dazzling thro' the leaves,
And flamed upon the brazen greaves
  Of bold Sir Lancelot.
A red-cross knight for ever kneel'd
To a lady in his shield,
That sparkled on the yellow field,
  Beside remote Shalott.

The gemmy bridle glitter'd free,
Like to some branch of stars we see
Hung in the golden Galaxy.
The bridle bells rang merrily
As he rode down to Camelot:
And from his blazon'd baldric slung
A mighty silver bugle hung,
And as he rode his armour rung,
Beside remote Shalott.

All in the blue unclouded weather
Thick-jewell'd shone the saddle-leather,
The helmet and the helmet-feather
Burn'd like one burning flame together,
As he rode down to Camelot.
As often thro' the purple night,
Below the starry clusters bright,
Some bearded meteor, trailing light,
Moves over still Shalott.

His broad clear brow in sunlight glow'd;
On burnish'd hooves his war-horse trode;
From underneath his helmet flow'd
His coal-black curls as on he rode,
As he rode down to Camelot.
From the bank and from the river
He flash'd into the crystal mirror,
"Tirra lirra," by the river
Sang Sir Lancelot.

She left the web, she left the loom,
She made three paces thro' the room,
She saw the water-lily bloom,
She saw the helmet and the plume,
She look'd down to Camelot.
Out flew the web and floated wide;
The mirror crack'd from side to side;
"The curse is come upon me," cried
The Lady of Shalott.

PART IV

In the stormy east-wind straining,
The pale yellow woods were waning,
The broad stream in his banks complaining,
Heavily the low sky raining
Over tower'd Camelot;
Down she came and found a boat
Beneath a willow left afloat,
And round about the prow she wrote
The Lady of Shalott.

And down the river's dim expanse –
Like some bold seer in a trance,
Seeing all his own mischance –
With a glassy countenance
Did she look to Camelot.
And at the closing of the day
She loosed the chain, and down she lay;
The broad stream bore her far away,
The Lady of Shalott.

Lying, robed in snowy white
That loosely flew to left and right –
The leaves upon her falling light –
Thro' the noises of the night
She floated down to Camelot:
And as the boat-head wound along
The willowy hills and fields among,
They heard her singing her last song.
The Lady of Shalott.

Heard a carol, mournful, holy,
Chanted loudly, chanted lowly,
Till her blood was frozen slowly,
And her eyes were darken'd wholly,
Turn'd to tower'd Camelot.
For ere she reach'd upon the tide
The first house by the water-side,
Singing in her song she died
The Lady of Shalott.

Under tower and balcony,
By garden-wall and gallery,
A gleaming shape she floated by,
Dead-pale between the houses high,
Silent into Camelot.
Out upon the wharfs they came,
Knight and burgher, lord and dame.
And round the prow they read her name,
The Lady of Shalott.

Who is this? and what is here?
And in the lighted palace near
Died the sound of royal cheer;
And they cross'd themselves for fear,
All the knights at Camelot:
But Lancelot mused a little space;
He said, "She has a lovely face;
God in his mercy lend her grace,
The Lady of Shalott."

Alfred, Lord Tennyson (1809–1892)

A Hymn in Praise of Neptune

Of Neptune's empire let us sing,
At whose command the waves obey;
To whom the rivers tribute pay,
Down the high mountains sliding:
To whom the scaly nation yields
Homage for the crystal fields
    Wherein they dwell:
And every sea-dog pays a gem
Yearly out of his wat'ry cell
To deck great Neptune's diadem.

The Tritons dancing in a ring
Before his palace gates do make
The water with their echoes quake,
Like the great thunder sounding:
The sea-nymphs chant their accents shrill,
And the sirens, taught to kill
    With their sweet voice,
Make ev'ry echoing rock reply
Unto their gentle murmuring noise
The praise of Neptune's empery.

Thomas Campion (1567–1620)

The Mermaid

I

Who would be
A mermaid fair,
Singing alone,
Combing her hair
Under the sea,
In a golden curl
With a comb of pearl,
On a throne?

II

I would be a mermaid fair;
I would sing to myself the whole of the day;
With a comb of pearl I would comb my hair;
And still as I comb'd I would sing and say,
'Who is it loves me? who loves not me?'
I would comb my hair till my ringlets would fall
                 Low adown, low adown,
From under my starry sea-bud crown
                 Low adown and around,
And I should look like a fountain of gold
                 Springing alone
            With a shrill inner sound,
              Over the throne
             In the midst of the hall;
Till that great sea-snake under the sea

From his coiled sleeps in the central deeps
Would slowly trail himself sevenfold
Round the hall where I sate, and look in at the gate
With his large calm eyes for the love of me.
And all the mermen under the sea
Would feel their immortality
Die in their hearts for the love of me.

III

But at night I would wander away, away,
        I would fling on each side my low-flowing
          locks,
And lightly vault from the throne and play
        With the mermen in and out of the rocks;
We would run to and fro, and hide and seek,
        On the broad sea-wolds in the crimson
          shells,
Whose silvery spikes are nighest the sea.
But if any came near I would call and shriek,
And adown the steep like a wave I would leap
        From the diamond-ledges that jut from the
          dells;
For I would not be kiss'd by all who would list,
Of the bold merry mermen under the sea.
They would sue me, and woo me, and flatter me,
In the purple twilights under the sea;
But the king of them all would carry me,
Woo me, and win me, and marry me,
In the branching jaspers under the sea.
Then all the dry-pied things that be

In the hueless mosses under the sea
Would curl round my silver feet silently,
All looking up for the love of me.
And if I should carol aloud, from aloft
All things that are forked, and horned, and soft
Would lean out from the hollow sphere of the sea,
All looking down for the love of me.

Alfred, Lord Tennyson (1809–1892)

The Merman

I

Who would be
A merman bold,
Sitting alone,
Singing alone
Under the sea,
With a crown of gold,
On a throne?

II

I would be a merman bold,
I would sit and sing the whole of the day;
I would fill the sea-halls with a voice of power;
But at night I would roam abroad and play
With the mermaids in and out of the rocks,
Dressing their hair with the white sea-flower;
And holding them back by their flowing locks
I would kiss them often under the sea,
And kiss them again till they kiss'd me
Laughingly, laughingly;
And then we would wander away, away,
To the pale-green sea-groves straight and high,
Chasing each other merrily.

III

There would be neither moon nor star;
But the wave would make music above us afar –
Low thunder and light in the magic night –
    Neither moon nor star.
We would call aloud in the dreamy dells,
Call to each other and whoop and cry
    All night, merrily, merrily.
They would pelt me with starry spangles and shells,
Laughing and clapping their hands between,
    All night, merrily, merrily,
But I would throw to them back in mine
Turkis and agate and almondine;
Then leaping out upon them unseen
I would kiss them often under the sea,
And kiss them again till they kiss'd me
    Laughingly, laughingly.
O, what a happy life were mine
Under the hollow-hung ocean green!
Soft are the moss-beds under the sea;
We would live merrily, merrily.

Alfred, Lord Tennyson (1809–1892)

The Forsaken Merman

Come, dear children, let us away;
Down and away below!
Now my brothers call from the bay,
Now the great winds shoreward blow,
Now the salt tides seaward flow;
Now the wild white horses play,
Champ and chafe and toss in the spray.
Children dear, let us away!
This way, this way!

Call her once before you go—
Call once yet!
In a voice that she will know:
'Margaret! Margaret!'
Children's voices should be dear
(Call once more) to a mother's ear;

Children's voices, wild with pain—
Surely she will come again!
Call her once and come away;
This way, this way!
'Mother dear, we cannot stay!
The wild white horses foam and fret.'
Margaret! Margaret!

Come, dear children, come away down;
Call no more!
One last look at the white-wall'd town
And the little grey church on the windy shore,

Then come down!
She will not come though you call all day;
Come away, come away!

Children dear, was it yesterday
We heard the sweet bells over the bay?
In the caverns where we lay,
Through the surf and through the swell,
The far-off sound of a silver bell?
Sand-strewn caverns, cool and deep,
Where the winds are all asleep;
Where the spent lights quiver and gleam,
Where the salt weed sways in the stream,
Where the sea-beasts, ranged all round,
Feed in the ooze of their pasture-ground;
Where the sea-snakes coil and twine,
Dry their mail and bask in the brine;
Where great whales come sailing by,
Sail and sail, with unshut eye,
Round the world for ever and aye?
When did music come this way?
Children dear, was it yesterday?

Children dear, was it yesterday
(Call yet once) that she went away?
Once she sate with you and me,
On a red gold throne in the heart of the sea,
And the youngest sate on her knee.
She comb'd its bright hair, and she tended it well,
When down swung the sound of a far-o bell.
She sigh'd, she look'd up through the clear
       green sea;
She said: 'I must go, to my kinsfolk pray
In the little grey church on the shore to-day.

'Twill be Easter-time in the world – ah me!
And I lose my poor soul, Merman! here with thee.'
I said: 'Go up, dear heart, through the waves;
Say thy prayer, and come back to the kind sea-caves!'
She smiled, she went up through the surf in the bay.
Children dear, was it yesterday?

Children dear, were we long alone?
'The sea grows stormy, the little ones moan;
Long prayers,' I said, 'in the world they say;
Come!' I said; and we rose through the surf in the bay.
We went up the beach, by the sandy down
Where the sea-stocks bloom, to the white-wall'd town;
Through the narrow paved streets, where all was still,
To the little grey church on the windy hill.
From the church came a murmur of folk at their
        prayers,
But we stood without in the cold blowing airs.
We climb'd on the graves, on the stones worn with
        rains,
And we gazed up the aisle through the small leaded
        panes.
She sate by the pillar; we saw her clear:
'Margaret, hist! come quick, we are here!
Dear heart,' I said, 'we are long alone;
The sea grows stormy, the little ones moan.'
But, ah, she gave me never a look,
For her eyes were seal'd to the holy book!
Loud prays the priest; shut stands the door.
Come away, children, call no more!

Come away, come down, call no more!
Down, down, down!
Down to the depths of the sea!

223

She sits at her wheel in the humming town,
Singing most joyfully.
Hark what she sings: 'O joy, O joy,
For the humming street, and the child with its toy!
For the priest, and the bell, and the holy well;
For the wheel where I spun,
And the blessed light of the sun!'
And so she sings her fill,
Singing most joyfully,
Till the spindle drops from her hand,
And the whizzing wheel stands still.
She steals to the window, and looks at the sand,
And over the sand at the sea;
And her eyes are set in a stare;
And anon there breaks a sigh,
And anon there drops a tear,
From a sorrow-clouded eye,
And a heart sorrow-laden,
A long, long sigh;
For the cold strange eyes of a little Mermaiden
And the gleam of her golden hair.

Come away, away children
Come children, come down!
The hoarse wind blows coldly;
Lights shine in the town.
She will start from her slumber
When gusts shake the door;
She will hear the winds howling,
Will hear the waves roar.
We shall see, while above us
The waves roar and whirl,
A ceiling of amber,
A pavement of pearl.

Singing: 'Here came a mortal,
But faithless was she!
And alone dwell for ever
The kings of the sea.'

But, children, at midnight,
When soft the winds blow,
When clear falls the moonlight,
When spring-tides are low;
When sweet airs come seaward
From heaths starr'd with broom,
And high rocks throw mildly
On the blanch'd sands a gloom;
Up the still, glistening beaches,
Up the creeks we will hie,
Over banks of bright seaweed
The ebb-tide leaves dry.
We will gaze, from the sand-hills,
At the white, sleeping town;
At the church on the hill-side—
And then come back down.
Singing: 'There dwells a loved one,
But cruel is she!
She left lonely for ever
The kings of the sea.'

Matthew Arnold (1822–1888)

Crossing the Bar

Sunset and evening star,
    And one clear call for me!
And may there be no moaning of the bar,
    When I put out to sea,

But such a tide as moving seems asleep,
    Too full for sound and foam,
When that which drew from out the boundless deep
    Turns again home.

Twilight and evening bell,
    And after that the dark!
And may there be no sadness of farewell,
    When I embark;

For though from out our bourne of Time and Place
    The flood may bear me far,
I hope to see my Pilot face to face
    When I have crossed the bar.

Alfred, Lord Tennyson (1809–1892)

Index of Poets

Index of Poets

Index of Titles

Index of Titles

Index of Titles

Index of First Lines

237

Permissions acknowledgements

The lines by T. S. Eliot on p. xx are from 'The Love Song of J. Alfred Prufrock', first published in *Poetry: A Magazine of Verse* in 1915 and collected in *Prufrock and Other Observations*, published by the Egoist Press in 1917.

'At Melville's Tomb', from *The Complete Poems of Hart Crane* by Hart Crane, edited by Marc Simon. Copyright 1933, 1958, 1966 by Liveright Publishing Corporation. Copyright © 1986 by Marc Simon. Used by permission of Liveright Publishing Corporation.

The Society of Authors as the Literary Representative of the Estate of John Masefield.

'It's the Sea I Want' in Elma Mitchell's *The Human Cage* (Peterloo Poets 1979).

Averill Curdy is the author of the poetry collection, *Song & Error* (Farrar, Straus, and Giroux).

MACMILLAN COLLECTOR'S LIBRARY

**Own the world's great works of literature in
one beautiful collectible library**

Designed and curated to appeal to book lovers everywhere,
Macmillan Collector's Library editions are small enough to
travel with you and striking enough to take pride of place
on your bookshelf. These much-loved literary classics
also make the perfect gift.

Beautifully produced with gilt edges, a ribbon marker,
bespoke illustrated cover and real cloth binding, every
Macmillan Collector's Library hardback adheres to the
same high production values.

Discover something new or cherish your favourite
stories with this elegant collection.

**Macmillan Collector's Library:
own, collect, and treasure**

Discover the full range at
macmillancollectorslibrary.com